"I'm sorry I bothered you.

"I'm even sorrier that it's getting dark and I have no idea how to get to my grandmother's house."

"You're only a hundred yards from her cottage. Turn right at the next road, and you can't miss it. Or maybe you can," Brian added under his breath.

"After all this time, you could've helped me, but you didn't say anything?" Amelia demanded. "I could've been out of here minutes ago."

"But then we wouldn't have had this interesting conversation," he said.

She should have thanked him or at least said goodbye, but her throat was dry and she was anxious to leave without any further incident. As she walked away, she didn't turn around to see if he was still standing there, still staring at her in that unsettling way he had. She didn't have to. She could feel his gaze on her as she retreated from his porch.

Dear Reader,

May has to be one of the most beautiful months of the year. Having been trapped indoors for the cold, dark winter, I love taking long walks and discovering new shops and restaurants that have opened in New York. And everywhere I turn, multicolored flowers line street medians; the sidewalks are flooded with baby carriages and the bridal salons lining Madison Avenue feature gowns that would make any woman feel like a princess.

As our special tribute to May, we've gathered romances from some of your favorite writers and from some pretty stellar new voices. Raye Morgan's BOARDROOM BRIDES continues with *The Boss's Special Delivery* (SR #1766). In this classic romance, a pregnant heroine finds love with her sworn enemy. Part of the FAIRY-TALE BRIDES continuity, *Beauty and the Big Bad Wolf* (SR #1767) by Carol Grace shows how an ambitious career woman falls for a handsome recluse. The next installment in Holly Jacobs's PERRY SQUARE miniseries, *Once Upon a Princess* (SR #1768), features a private investigator who's decided it's time a runaway princess came home…to him! Finally, two single parents get a second chance at love, in Lissa Manley's endearing romance *In a Cowboy's Arms* (SR #1769).

And be sure to come back next month when Patricia Thayer and Lilian Darcy return to the line.

Ann Leslie Tuttle
Associate Senior Editor

Please address questions and book requests to:
Silhouette Reader Service
U.S.: 3010 Walden Ave., P.O. Box 1325, Buffalo, NY 14269
Canadian: P.O. Box 609, Fort Erie, Ont. L2A 5X3

Beauty
and the
Big Bad Wolf

CAROL GRACE

Published by Silhouette Books

America's Publisher of Contemporary Romance

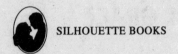 SILHOUETTE BOOKS

ISBN 0-373-19767-5

BEAUTY AND THE BIG BAD WOLF

Copyright © 2005 by Carol Culver

This edition published by arrangement with Harlequin Books S.A.

® and TM are trademarks of Harlequin Books S.A., used under license.
Trademarks indicated with ® are registered in the United States Patent
and Trademark Office, the Canadian Trade Marks Office and in other
countries.

Visit Silhouette Books at www.eHarlequin.com

Printed in U.S.A.

Books by Carol Grace

CAROL GRACE

has always been interested in travel and living abroad. She spent her junior year of college in France and toured the world working on the hospital ship *HOPE*. She and her husband spent the first year and a half of their marriage in Iran, where they both taught English. She has studied Arabic and Persian languages. Then, with their toddler daughter, they lived in Algeria for two years.

Carol says that writing is another way of making her life exciting. Her office is her mountaintop home, which overlooks the Pacific Ocean and which she shares with her inventor husband, their daughter, who just graduated from college, and their teenage son.

For my wonderful, smart nephew David Warme,
whose inventive mind will lead to great things!
This book is for you, with love from Aunt Carol.

Chapter One

Amelia Tucker drove as fast as she dared up and down the mountain roads that led to her grandmother's house in the woods. She was late. She was worried. Worried about Granny's health, worried about her job and worried about what she'd say to the man who'd just proposed to her when she'd left San Francisco that morning.

She was annoyed when her cell-phone battery conked out in the middle of an important call, but that was no excuse for missing the turn and ending up in the driveway of a huge glass-and-redwood house with Do Not Disturb and Beware of Dog signs on the fence.

Now she was not only late and worried, she was

lost, too. It was dusk, and the trees were casting shadows across roads that all looked alike. She got out of her car and paused long enough to inhale the pungent scent of pine and fir trees. Very gingerly, she approached the fence, expecting a ferocious dog to come leaping over it and tear her to shreds at any minute. She knocked on the gate, but nothing happened. No barking, no snarling, no growling. No dog.

Feeling bold and reassured, she opened the gate and stepped onto a flagstone walkway.

"Hello," she called into the silence. "Anybody home?" If only she could borrow the phone to call Granny or get directions. She couldn't be far, and everybody knew everybody in these mountain communities.

Hearing no answer, Amelia walked up to the redwood deck and peered into a huge window. Staring back at from the other side of the window was a tall, good-looking man. Startled, she froze and stared back. His dark eyes held her gaze for a long moment. She tried to look away, but couldn't. What was it about him that made chills go up her spine? Sure, he was handsome in a rugged kind of way, or at least he would be without that angry frown on his face. She teetered back on her heels for a moment, uncertain how to proceed.

Then she waved her hand and smiled. She hadn't risen to executive status in an up-and-coming soft-

ware company by letting handsome, angry men in-
timidate her.

"Didn't you see the sign?" he said gruffly.

"Yes, but—"

"Then go away."

Had she heard that right? Had the man really told
her to go away? "Wait, I'm not selling anything or trying to convert you. I just want to ask you something."

Suddenly, the front door flew open and the man
stalked out on the deck, followed by a huge yellow
Labrador happily wagging its tail. The contrast between the two, the friendly dog and the decidedly unfriendly man, was startling. The guy was bigger than
she'd thought, looming over her five feet nine inches,
making her feel small and insignificant for the first
time in…well, forever. She, who had everything in
her life under control, who was on a mission of
mercy, was being intimidated by some guy with
broad shoulders, a craggy face and an imposing, lord-
of-the-manor attitude. Of all the cabins and summer
cottages in these woods, why, oh why, had she
stopped here?

"Didn't you see the sign?" he repeated, as if she
were mentally deficient or illiterate, or both.

"The one that said Beware of Dog?"

"The one that said Do Not Disturb."

"Yes, but I have a question," she said with what
she hoped was a disarming smile. What was it

Granny always said about catching more flies with honey? Good grief, what she had to do to get a little information out of him!

He didn't return her smile. His mouth was set in a hard line. She had the feeling he didn't smile very often, if ever. Maybe that was even a hint of sadness lurking in the depths of his dark blue eyes. If it was, it was no excuse for being rude and had nothing to do with her. She probably ought to take the hint and get out of here right now. But not until she found out how to get to Granny's.

She knew she should get right to the point and leave the premises, but for some reason, she continued to engage in the ridiculous conversation. There was something about the man that bothered and intrigued her. Why was he holed up here, behind a tall fence with a bunch of warning signs on it?

"If you really don't want to be disturbed, maybe you should get a bigger sign or a scarier dog." She thought about petting the dog just to show she was a nice, friendly person, but for all she knew, he would command it to attack her and chase her from the place. She'd never had a dog or a pet of any kind and knew nothing about them. The dog, perhaps sensing her innocence, licked her hand and wagged its tail even more happily.

"Most people respect my privacy," he said, giving her a long, slow look, from her up-to-the-minute hairstyle to the tips of her Italian leather shoes. What was that glance about? Surely not appreciation for her carefully assembled ensemble, was it?

His gaze warmed for a moment and made her break out in goose bumps. Another first. It must be the altitude, or the early evening breeze that blew through the pine trees. She could deal with anything the most flirtatious men came up with, both in and out of her office, but this man was not flirting. He was just looking, practically glaring, and taking his time about it. Sure, she was a stranger, and he didn't want strangers around, but what was his damage? "I'm sorry, but I didn't think you'd mind," she said.

"Obviously. If this keeps up, I'll have to install an electronic fence to zap intruders." He couldn't be serious, could he? He sounded serious. And he certainly looked serious.

"That sounds a little extreme," she said with a little shiver as she felt an imaginary zing course through her body. "Look, Mr.…whoever you are—"

"No, you look, Ms. whoever *you* are," he said, his jaw tight and his eyes clear and cool. "I don't want to buy anything or give any interviews. So take your questions and go peddle your products elsewhere and leave the premises."

"Or you'll do what—sic your ferocious dog on me?"

He glanced down at the dog, who appeared to be following their conversation by turning his head from side to side. "Some watchdog," he muttered. "Some days, you don't earn your keep."

Surely a man with a friendly dog wouldn't take drastic measures to make her leave, such as tossing her over the fence, but it was time to try the direct approach. "If it's not too much trouble," she said sweetly, "I just need a little help, and I only have one question—where am I?"

"You're in Pine Mountain, California, five miles off Highway 80. Next time, I suggest you install a GPS in your car. Now will you please leave?"

"Yes… No! I'm trying to find my grandmother's house."

His eyes narrowed as he looked her over again this time, his gaze lingering much longer than necessary on the lines of her fitted black business suit, sending a shaft of sensual awareness through her body. What was wrong with her? What was wrong with him? She might look out of place here in the country, but she certainly looked harmless, and she'd made it clear she was lost and only needed directions.

"Grandmother's house," he repeated, jerking his gaze away at last. This time, the corner of his mouth lifted just a fraction. "Who are you, Little Red Riding Hood?"

"If you're referring to my hair," Amelia began, trying to think of a retort. She usually had one ready, having been teased about her red hair more times than she cared to remember. But for the life of her, she couldn't think of anything suitable to say at that moment. She blamed it on the short but stressful day at the office followed by the long drive here. But it wasn't only that. It was him. Him and the way he looked at her, hot then cold. Nervously, she ran her hand through her hair.

Her head was spinning. It would be dark soon and Granny would be getting worried about her. The guy was standing there, staring at her, waiting for her to finish her sentence, which she wasn't going to do. Why should she? What did it matter what she said, or didn't say? Someday, someone would put him in his place, but it wasn't going to be her, and it wasn't going to be today.

He had problems—like paranoia and hostility— but she didn't want to hear about them or deal with them. They had nothing to do with her. She was out of here. Now. Forget using his phone. Forget getting anything useful out of him. Forget wondering why he was hiding away from the world on this beautiful piece of property, in this stunning, custom-built house.

He was casually dressed in khakis and a polo shirt. Leisure wear or work clothes? Home office? Vacation house? Illegal crop growing?

She told herself it was none of her business. Yes, he appeared to have money and good looks, but how he had succeeded in business with his bad attitude was a mystery—and a mystery it would stay. All she wanted was to be on her way. She had Granny to take care of and work to do. She needed to get out now, before she gave in to her abundant natural curiosity and tried to find out what made him tick.

"Never mind," she said, finding her voice and her determination at last. "I'll find Granny's house on my own." She turned on her heel and spun around, but when she tried to walk away, she couldn't. Her heel was caught in a crack between the redwood boards of the deck.

"Damn," she said under her breath.

He sighed loudly, as if he were at the end of his rope. "I'll get it," he said, bending down to grab the heel of the shoe. Before she could step out of her shoe, he got down on his knees and put one hand around her ankle. Shocked by the warmth of his strong grip, she sucked in a sharp breath. He yanked, and the heel separated from her shoe. She put her hand out and grabbed his shoulder to keep from stumbling. He looked up at her, and their eyes met and held for a long moment. There was hostility in his gaze, but there was something else in that guarded look, something that made her pulse speed up.

Strangely shaken, she dragged her gaze away and looked at her shoe. "Oh, no. Do you know how much these shoes cost?"

He straightened, holding the heel in his hand. "I can guess," he said.

"Look," she said, standing awkwardly in one shoe and one stockinged foot. "I'm sorry I bothered you. I'm sorry I interrupted your life. I'm even sorrier that it's getting dark and I have no idea how to get to my grandmother's house."

"Is your grandmother Helen Wickett?" he asked. "If she is, you're only one hundred yards from her cottage. Turn right at the next road, and you can't miss it. Or maybe you can," he added under his breath.

"After all this time, you guessed who she was, and you didn't say anything?" she demanded. "I could have been out of here minutes ago."

"But then we wouldn't have had this interesting conversation," he said.

"I'm no stranger to sarcasm," she replied. She still didn't understand why he couldn't have told her where she was ten minutes ago. She only knew she hoped she'd never see him again. He was a combination of unusual traits, all of which she found disturbing and off-putting. This was not a good time in her life for her to be disturbed by a strange man.

When he handed her the detached heel, his hand brushed hers, and she felt the kind of zing she expected from an electric fence. Amelia saw something flicker in his gaze, which made her think he'd felt it, too. But that wasn't possible. Not him. Not here. Not her.

She should have thanked him, or at least said goodbye, but her throat was dry and she was anxious to leave without any further incident. So she turned and walked back out the gate to her car, shoulders back, head held high, both shoes in hand as the rough flagstones tore holes in the soles of her sheer stockings. But she didn't turn around to see if he was still standing there, still staring at her in that unsettling way he had. She didn't have to. She could feel his gaze on her as she retreated from his porch.

A few minutes later, Amelia was at the door of the small, charming cottage in the midst of a pine grove, her computer in one hand, her small suitcase in the other. Once she was inside the snug living room, surrounded by familiar, old-fashioned furniture and the warmth of a wood-burning stove, she hugged her grandmother, who was stretched on a long, slipcovered couch and wearing a pink chenille bathrobe.

"I was worried about you," Helen said, kissing Amelia on the cheek.

"I got a late start, and then I took a wrong turn. And when I tried to call you, my phone went dead. But here I am. How are you feeling?"

"Not bad for an old lady with one titanium hip," she said cheerfully, patting her hip that was covered with a cast. "I feel helpless for the first time in my life, and I just hate having to ask you to help out this way, but my sister Vivian was busy and Marge came down with the flu. I didn't know who else to ask."

"You should have asked me first. Of course, I'm sorry about your hip, but I love having an excuse to spend some time here. It's so peaceful and quiet." Maybe just a little too quiet for a city girl who lived, worked and breathed her job. Amelia was used to the noise and activity and excitement of the urban scene. But she'd only be here for a week—two weeks at most. "It will be like a vacation," she added. A vacation she couldn't afford to take right now, with everything that was going on at the office. But Granny's health had to come first.

"I hope so. I don't want to be a burden. Of course, I have the home-help workers, but they only come three times a week."

"And they're not family. You can't tell them what to do, the way you can me," she said with a smile.

"Now, Amelia, I may have told you what to do when you were a child, but you always did it your own way." Her granny's eyes twinkled, but Amelia knew she meant what she'd said. Amelia'd heard she had a stubborn streak more than once over the years.

And one thing she would stubbornly refuse to do was let her grandmother guess this was the absolute worst time for Amelia to be away from the office. The company's software writers were asking for more pay, the board of directors was demanding to see higher profits and she was going to have to lay off some of her favorite people. And if the business didn't improve, she'd have to come up with a new business plan.

On top of that, her boyfriend Jeff was pressing her for a commitment. If she married him, she wouldn't have to worry about a job. He'd support her. But she didn't want to simply be taken care of. She was an achiever, determined to succeed on her own. And that meant she couldn't afford to take one day off, let alone a week. But her grandmother needed her, and so she came.

"You look tired, dear," her grandmother said, peering at Amelia over her bifocals.

"Maybe just a little." She was always tired these days, but she'd learned to live with it.

"You work too hard."

Too hard? Was there such a thing? "What would I do if I didn't work hard?" she asked. "Watch soap operas? Shop? Do lunch?"

"I was thinking more of something like gardening, cooking or walking in the woods."

Amelia smiled. "Maybe when I'm retired, like you. For now, I'm on track. I have certain goals and objectives. I thought by now…" She broke off before she got started on her plans for the future. The future, always there, full of possibilities, always right around the corner, but always just out of her grasp.

"Does this have anything to do with your parents?" Granny asked with a frown. Granny made no secret of the fact that she disapproved of the rigid all-work-and-no-play, goal-oriented lifestyle Amelia had been brought up with.

"I suppose their advice is always there in the back of my head—push forward, get to the top, let nothing stand in your way—sure. But I like to think they're *my* goals, and not theirs."

"I'm sure they are," Granny said calmly.

"Something smells good," Amelia said, eager to change the subject. "You haven't been cooking, have you?"

"I made a lasagna before I went in for surgery," Helen said. "I took it out of the freezer and hobbled over to put it in the oven tonight."

"I could have put it in for you. You have to stay off your feet. I'll go wash up and change into something comfortable."

"Same room, top of the stairs," Helen said. "Where are your shoes?"

"Oh, uh, here in my bag." No use going into what happened. Why start off by complaining about one of her neighbors? Though maybe Granny knew what his story was. If anyone knew, it would be her. She could inspire confidence in the shiest bachelor or the most hardened con man.

Amelia told herself to forget Granny's surly

neighbor. He'd certainly forgotten her, though she couldn't imagine many others who'd penetrated his fence, and his warnings, and actually gotten inside the compound. Maybe that explained why he'd glared at her as though she were an alien from outer space—he didn't see that many strangers.

She quickly plugged in her laptop, recharged her phone battery and checked her messages. In the small upstairs bathroom with the whitewashed walls, she scrubbed the makeup off her face, ran her hands through her hair, then changed into faded jeans and a T-shirt.

From the top of the stairs, she heard voices from below. Her granny's voice and a man's voice. She frowned. Oh, dear. Would she have to make polite conversation with some yokel? Yes, if he was a friend of Granny's. Should she change? No, she was in the country now. It was probably one of the geezers from the local garden club who wouldn't notice what she was wearing.

"I stacked the firewood out on your deck," Brian Wolf said as he stepped into Helen's living room. He'd just seen the fancy British sports car in front of the house, but Ms. "Do you know how much these shoes cost?" was nowhere to be seen, fortunately. If he could get out of here without encountering her, he'd count himself lucky. If Helen hadn't just called to say she was desperately in need of firewood, he would have waited to come by until he was sure the red-haired hotshot was gone. "You're not really out of firewood. There's quite a pile out there."

"Oh, is there? I didn't see it," Helen said, her faded blue eyes wide and innocent. "You'll have to forgive an old lady. My eyesight is fading along with everything else. Oh, you brought Dante. Come here, you sweet boy."

Brian watched his "ferocious" watchdog wag his tail and take his place by Helen's side so she could lavish attention on him.

"Call me anytime," he said. "You know I can use the exercise. Before I go, wasn't there something you wanted done in your greenhouse?"

"Oh, yes. My potted Meyer lemon tree has to be moved. It's not getting enough sun where it is. But it can wait…for a few minutes. Actually, it takes two to move it. My granddaughter Amelia just arrived, and she'll be downstairs in a minute to help you."

Oh, no. He was stuck with another encounter with Helen's granddaughter, who was just exactly what he'd imagined from her descriptions—sophisticated, well-dressed, snotty, aloof, cool and sure of herself. He knew the type only too well. The only thing that had surprised him was the rich color of her hair. The photographs he'd seen of her were black and white.

In the late afternoon sun filtered through the trees, it had shone like a copper penny, almost blinding him.

"Amelia," Helen called. "Come on down. We have company."

"If she's busy, I can come back another day." He eyed the front door, thinking of making a run for it.

"She's not busy at all. She's here to take care of me. Isn't that sweet, giving up her vacation to spend it with me? Honestly, she's the kindest, sweetest, nicest girl in the world. Pretty and smart, too."

"I'm sure she is," he said politely, though he was sure what he was hearing was grandmother-speak.

"Just sit down. She'll be right down. You two have a lot in common."

"You think so?" Brian asked, unable to conceal the skepticism in his voice, while bracing one hip against the wall near the door.

"I know so. You're both capable and hardworking."

Hardworking? He hadn't felt like working for almost a year now—ever since his life had fallen apart late one Saturday night on a mountain road. Hard worker or not, he did not want to have any more to do with Ms. High-and-Mighty. He'd rather stay buried in the woods, alone with his dog and his thoughts. On the other hand, he didn't want to disappoint Helen. She was one hell of a wonderful woman—independent, self-sufficient, warm and generous. She deserved better than that fiery, arrogant granddaughter. But for Helen's sake, he'd try to be polite to her.

"Amelia is quite an amazing girl," Helen said. "A wonderful cook, a brilliant executive…"

"Granny." Amelia's voice came wafting down the stairs. "Are you talking about me again?" The startled look on her face as she reached the bottom step was almost priceless. She stopped dead in her tracks when she saw the dog, and she knew instantly who the visitor was. Her gaze flew from the dog to the man, and she stared openmouthed at him, gripping the back of a chair as if she were in danger of falling down. He smothered a grin while Helen introduced him. If he gave in to that kind of impulse, and really smiled, he was afraid his face might crack.

"Amelia, I want you to meet my neighbor, Brian Wolf. And this is his dog, Dante. Honestly, if I ever get a dog, I'd want one just like this. I've told you about Brian and his dog, haven't I?"

"I…I don't think so, no," she murmured.

If she'd known he was there, Brian was sure she would have made up some excuse to stay in her room until he'd left. But it was too late. She forced a smile and held out her hand to shake his. *Don't worry, sweetheart, I'm just as sorry as you are that your grandmother is trying to match us up, but as soon as we move the lemon tree, I'm out of here, and we won't have to see each other again. So buck up, smile and shake hands. If I can stand it, so can you.*

"Nice to meet you," he said, noting that she'd changed out of her city clothes into something more suitable for country life. He'd bet that in the city she never wore that old cotton T-shirt that hugged her breasts. He shouldn't be staring, but he told himself he was only trying to figure out the faded logo. Faded or not, she still smelled of some expensive perfume, and she didn't fool him. She could wear whatever she wanted—denims or an apron, dungarees and a straw hat—she was still a city woman, with expensive shoes, a hairstylist, waxed eyebrows, an analyst and a personal trainer. Yes, he knew the type. All sharp edges and high expectations. He'd had enough city women—one was enough to last a lifetime—to know that they didn't fit into country life. He'd give this one a few days before she made up some excuse and headed back to town.

"I've heard so much about you," he said, his voice sharper than he'd intended. "It's too bad you had to wait for a crisis to come and visit."

Amelia flushed, and he was almost sorry he'd criticized her, but not completely. Where *had* she been all this time? He'd lived here for almost two years, and as far as he knew, she'd never visited her grandmother.

"Now, Brian," Helen said reprovingly. "Amelia is a very busy person. She's the head of her company, aren't you, dear?"

"Not quite yet, Granny."

"Well, you soon will be. Only, you're looking peaked. Isn't she, Brian?"

"She looks fine to me," he said gallantly. What else could he say with her grandmother sitting across the room? "You don't often see that color hair," he added gratuitously. He was rewarded for that remark by a hostile glare from Amelia.

"Beautiful, just beautiful," Helen .enthused. "Comes from my side of the family. My sister Ruth had hair that same color. She was a beauty, too, just like you," she said to her granddaughter. Amelia blushed, which surprised him. He would have thought she was much too sophisticated to blush at a compliment.

Amelia quickly changed the subject. "How are your orchids doing, Granny?"

Helen reported that she'd been given a new phalaenopsis while in the hospital, and it, along with her other plants, was in the greenhouse in the back. "Which reminds me," she said. "Brian has offered to move my Meyer lemon tree for me. If you'll give him a hand, I'd really appreciate it. It's getting too much sun where it is, and the leaves are looking brown."

"I thought it needed more sun," Brian said.

"Did I say that?" Helen said with a little laugh. "I must be getting senile. Amelia will know where it should go."

"But I don't really know..." Amelia said.

"Thank you, dear. Dante can stay here with me."

What could she say to that suggestion? Nothing. Brian followed Amelia out the back door in total silence. He couldn't help noticing how her faded jeans hugged her hips. So she didn't dress like the busy executive every minute, even though she acted like one. If she didn't have such a pained look on her face, if she didn't purse her lips as if she'd just bitten into one of Helen's Meyer lemons, she wouldn't be hard to look at. As if it mattered. What mattered was she never visited her grandmother, and would have continued to ignore her if it weren't for Helen's hip surgery.

He didn't really care what this woman looked like as long as she took good care of her grandmother. As for him, he had nothing to say to her, and she obviously had nothing to say to him. In the small, glassed-in greenhouse, the air was damp and humid, the scent was rich and earthy. The orchids were lush, fragrant and sexy. The silence and the atmosphere were closing in on him and getting on his nerves. He looked around for a lemon tree, but he didn't see one. Was this whole thing a setup? He wanted to leave, but he owed it to Helen to be polite to her granddaughter.

He braced one arm against a wooden shelf. "So tell me, Red, what is it your company does?" he asked.

"First," she said, her chin tilted at an upward angle, "it isn't *my* company. The company I work for makes software for medical use. And second, no one calls me Red."

"Why not?" he asked. He couldn't help admiring the way her rich auburn hair shone under the bare bulb hanging from the ceiling. He took his finger, wound a strand of hair around it and examined it closely. "Is it because it isn't real?" Pushing her buttons was so easy.

She glared at him and stepped backward. He dropped his hand to his side. She looked so mad, he thought she might spit fire like a dragon. "Just kidding," he said lightly.

"And what is it you do, Mr. Wolf?" she asked icily.

"Nothing," he said. Damn, why had he started this line of inquiry? Now the tables were turned, and he wanted no part of it.

"Nothing," she repeated, shaking her head in disbelief. "Then why do you need all that security around your house? I assumed you were developing a secret weapon or, at least, a cure for cancer."

"Don't ever assume anything about me," he said brusquely. "Chances are, you'd be wrong."

"Don't tell me what to do," she said stiffly. "I didn't just fall off a turnip truck."

"No," he said, taking advantage of the remark to take another look at her long, lithe body. "I didn't think so."

"Do you mean you're retired?"

"Not really," he said, watching the way her eyes narrowed and her lower lip stuck out when she was annoyed. He wondered if she ever smiled. Not that he cared. It was not his job to coax a smile out of an uptight visitor. He really didn't care if she ever cracked a smile. "Do you have any more questions, because if not…"

"Just one. Are all the neighbors as unfriendly as you?"

"You'll have to ask your grandmother," he said. "I like to think I stand out from the crowd."

"I'm sure you do," she said.

"I have a feeling that's not a compliment," he said drily.

"You're very perceptive."

"Why, Red, that's the first nice thing you've said to me," he drawled sarcastically.

She looked at him as if he'd crawled out from under a rock. "I should be getting back to the kitchen."

"What about the lemon tree?" he asked. Truthfully, he'd almost forgotten about it himself. Was he that desperate for company that he was almost enjoying this banter? No way.

She looked around and pointed to a short, stubby tree with shiny leaves, planted in a ceramic pot. She took one side and he took the other, and they moved it close to the slanted glass wall. His hand brushed

hers as they set it down, and he felt a jolt of awareness so strong he dropped his side of the pot a little
too soon. He jerked his hand away and stuffed it in
his pocket. She shot him a puzzled look, but didn't
question his abrupt reaction.

Brian knew what his problem was. *Too much
time alone. Too much time without a woman.* On the
other hand, he had no intention of getting involved
with a woman again. He'd learned his lesson the
hard way.

Without saying another word, they went back into
the house. Even though she was cynical and sarcas-
tic, stiff and untouchable, he kind of hated to go back
in because it would be interesting to see what she'd
say next. She was capable of putting him down and
challenging him with her questions. It was a surpris-
ingly welcome change from all the sycophants who
turned up in his driveway to tell him how brilliant and
original he was, to plead with him to get back to
work and finish what he'd started or to hear what his
next project would be. She knew nothing about
him—he was a clean slate—and frankly, she didn't
seem that interested in finding out any more.

Which was fine with him. The feeling was mutual.
He didn't want to see any more of her after tonight.
If someday he did decide to rejoin the world, as
Helen often suggested, and he had to find a woman,
he'd choose the company of some sweet, soft-spo-

ken, sympathetic woman. For now, and for the foreseeable future, he intended to keep away from Ms. Amelia Tucker. The sooner the better.

Chapter Two

Back at the house, the rich smell of tomato sauce and cheese filled the air. Brian hadn't realized how hungry he was. He hoped it didn't show on his face, because even imminent starvation wouldn't be reason enough to sit through dinner with Amelia. He'd done his bit. He'd been polite. They'd exchanged a few pointed remarks. There was no love lost between them. That was it.

"You *will* stay for dinner," Helen said.

"I wish I could," he said, making an effort to sound sincere, "but I have to get back. Something urgent has come up." He managed a polite smile, and before Helen could press him about what was so urgent, Brian quickly said goodbye, whistled for his dog and walked out the front door. He felt guilty seeing the disappointment on the old lady's face, but he didn't want to give Helen any more ideas about throwing him and her granddaughter together.

If he ran into Amelia again, he might be able to summon the energy to say he was sorry for his boorish behavior that afternoon. If he'd known who she was, he never would have acted that way, out of respect to Helen. But how was he to know she wasn't another journalist after a big story? Or just a curious passerby who'd read about him? Or even one of his fans? Though, admittedly she wasn't the type. He'd had enough publicity and intruders to last a lifetime. He couldn't be vigilant enough, nor rude enough, to scare them all away. But he'd keep trying.

Amelia never thought the man would stay for dinner, but she knew Granny would invite him. She breathed a huge sigh of relief when he declined and left with his dog. She did not feel the least bit let down. What she did feel was fatigue. It had been a long day, a long drive and then—him. Of course she was curious about him. Who wouldn't be? But it was clear he wasn't about to divulge any secrets—such as what he did or why he needed those buffers between him and the world.

"You and Brian have so much in common," Helen

said when Amelia had set up her tray on the couch and served her a large helping of lasagna.

"Really? I can't imagine what that would be," Amelia said from her chair at the small dining table.

"You're both successful businesspeople, something I could never be," Helen said with a modest smile. "I was only a simple housewife."

"Granny," Amelia said, setting her fork down. "You were never a simple anything. You were the world's greatest grandmother—self-sufficient and talented. You taught me so much—how to make an apple pie, how to knit, how to prune roses, how to plant carrots and potatoes…not that I have time for that kind of thing anymore, but still. As for your neighbor, he told me he doesn't do anything."

Helen laughed merrily, as if Amelia'd told a joke. "He's such a tease. It is true that Brian's been taking a well-deserved break."

"From…?" Amelia asked, hoping she didn't sound too interested. After all, she was just making conversation. If Granny wanted to talk about her neighbor, who was Amelia to stop her?

"From his business," Granny said. "He sometimes seems reticent, but when you get to know him, I'm sure he'll tell you all about it."

"That would be lovely," Amelia said, knowing that would never happen. "But I'm going to be busy taking care of you." And getting some work done whenever she could. "I doubt I'll have time for any socializing."

"Oh, nonsense," Helen said. "I can't have you cooped up here with me all the time. You'll be bored silly. It will do you good to get out and smell the roses."

"I can smell them from here," Amelia said. "Unless you've torn out your Lady Bird Johnson hybrids."

"Oh, no. Which reminds me—I need some plant food from the hardware store in town. If you get a chance sometime this week, maybe you could run in and pick some up?"

"Of course. I'll go tomorrow. I need a few things myself."

"You'll hardly recognize the place. They've added a complete housewares section. The whole town is talking about it."

"Really?" Amelia wondered whether, if she lived here, she'd get excited about some small-town store expanding. It boggled her mind to think her life might be reduced to that.

"I know what you're thinking," Granny said. "This is nothing compared to San Francisco, where you can get anything you want anytime of day or night. But there are some advantages to living in the country."

"Of course there are. I never said—"

"But you thought it." As usual, Helen could see right through her. When her grandmother put her fork down and folded her napkin, Amelia jumped up and removed her plate. "Sit down and relax and tell me what's happening in your life these days," Granny said, putting her hand on Amelia's arm. "It's been so long since we've had a good talk."

Amelia sneaked a glance at her watch. She had planned to set up her fax machine and check her messages, but she couldn't go now without seeming abrupt. She'd just have to wait. Surely Granny would go to bed early.

"How about some coffee?" Amelia asked. "I brought my espresso machine."

"Oh, my, that sounds wonderful. Wait until Brian hears that. He's quite a coffee drinker. He'll be sorry he didn't stay for dinner."

"I'm sure he will," Amelia said. "I bet he's kicking himself right now for rushing away when he could have had the pleasure of our company, not to mention your excellent lasagna."

Her grandmother gave her a knowing smile that said she was no stranger to sarcasm, either, before Amelia went out to her car to get her coffeemaker as well as her fax machine. Granny was so very anxious that her granddaughter and her neighbor get along, Amelia didn't have the heart to dampen her enthusiasm. She'd realize soon enough that it wasn't meant to be.

In a few minutes, Amelia was frothing milk and making decaf lattes. Her grandmother exclaimed at how clever she was to come up with such a novel drink. Trying to ignore the fax machine she'd set on the floor, which reminded her of all the work she had to do, Amelia curled up in the large overstuffed armchair, put her coffee on the table next to her and tucked her bare feet under her.

"My life is…well, things are kind of hectic these days."

Her grandmother nodded. "No time for fun?"

"I enjoy my work," Amelia said, conscious of how dull that must sound. "It's interesting and exciting and full of possibilities." There, that sounded good. Even Granny would have to admit it. Hadn't she just been bragging to that man about how accomplished as well as beautiful Amelia was? It made her blush all over again to think about it.

"Yes, but don't forget that on their deathbed, no one ever says they wish they'd spent more time at the office. Not that you're anywhere near your deathbed."

"I hope not." Amelia stifled a yawn. It was only eight-thirty, but her eyelids were heavy and her brain seemed to have shut down. It must be the air or the altitude. She had hours of work to do, and she never went to bed before midnight at home. Then she was usually up at six for a workout at the health club before work.

"You're tired. You go on up to bed," Granny said.

Amelia got Granny's medicine, helped her into the

bathroom and settled her in for the night. After kissing her grandmother good-night, she picked up her fax machine and started upstairs.

"Amelia?"

"Yes, Granny?"

"I'm glad you're here."

"So am I."

But in the small bedroom at the top of the stairs, Amelia couldn't help thinking of what she'd be doing if she were at home. On Friday nights, a group from the office went out for sushi on Union Street. Because of all the bars and upscale restaurants, parking would be scarce and the sidewalks would be crowded with young professionals like herself. She'd probably run into friends, and they'd end up at a Starbucks, talking shop. The city was energizing, and being in the country had mellowed her so much, she couldn't seem to function. Tomorrow she'd be back on track.

She plugged in her fax machine and charged the battery to her cell phone. But she didn't check her messages. She looked around the room, with its flowered wallpaper and rolltop desk that had belonged to her grandfather, and the memories came flooding back. When she'd been a little girl, she'd been sent to Granny's for the summer so her overachiever parents could go off on research projects to the far corners of the earth. She'd spent many happy hours in the kitchen with Granny, making wild-strawberry jam, rolling piecrust or picking wildflowers in the woods and pressing them between waxed paper. She always looked forward to summer at Granny's. Fall meant a return to school and a structured routine.

Yes, even if she had to stay here for two weeks, she owed Granny that much, and more. Her grandmother had been there when Amelia had needed her, and now Granny needed Amelia. Instead of setting up her computer, checking her messages and sending off a few faxes, Amelia slipped into her nightgown, crawled between the flannel sheets and fell sound asleep just as the grandfather clock downstairs struck ten.

A few hours later, the hooting of an owl woke her up. She, who could sleep through sirens and garbage trucks, had been awakened by a bird. She went to the window and looked out through the trees. In the distance, there was a light shining. From the neighbor's house? What was his name—Wolf? If he didn't work, why would he still be up? Maybe he was hunched over his computer, writing mystery novels. Or maybe he was in an online chat room, talking to Russian mail-order brides. Maybe he was doing something illegal, such as making moonshine liquor. Or maybe he was ordering tighter security equipment on eBay. None of her business, she thought, as she firmly closed the window and went back to bed.

But now her mind was spinning, thinking about the mystery man. And the images kept rolling through her sleepless brain until finally, mercifully, her brain shut off and she fell asleep.

The next morning, Amelia opened the bedroom window and shivered in her sheer nightgown in the cool morning air. There in the distance was the out-line of a large house—the house where the occupant was a night owl. She assumed it was the same house she'd stopped at last night. She'd had no idea it was so close. Though it was a mile or two by the road, it was only a hundred yards or so through the woods, as he'd said. The house was much too close for comfort. Though she was sure Brian was just as eager to avoid any further contact with her as she was with him.

What did her grandmother see in him? He was ar-rogant, obnoxious and overbearing. Perhaps in the country, one got desperate for company. And of course he was helpful and nice to her, on hand to move heavy objects or whatever. Amelia was glad to say she'd never be that desperate for help or company.

After sleeping fitfully, she was still tired, but she had work to do. If she were at home, she'd go for a run on the Marina Green then head into the office, though it was Saturday. She'd get caught up when no one else was there. Jeff wouldn't mind. He worked on the weekends, too. They had so much in common. Maybe that was enough for a good marriage.

She was so lost in her thoughts, she didn't hear the truck pull up until it was too late. Brian Wolf got out and stood on the gravel driveway, looking up at her. Their eyes met briefly, and she shivered again before she slammed the window shut and got dressed. She gave a sigh of relief when she heard the truck's engine start. He could have seen right through her sheer nightgown, if he'd wanted to—which he probably didn't, so why was she so upset about nothing? He'd been there last night and then first thing in the morning. If this was his pattern, how was she going to avoid him?

Her grandmother was alone downstairs. Amelia greeted her with a kiss and got her pills for her. She didn't even glance out the window or ask any questions. She didn't want to know why Brian had returned this morning, when he couldn't get out of here fast enough last night. She fixed toast and coffee for her grandmother, and together they made a shopping list. Halfway through it, Helen paused.

"What did you think of Brian?" she asked lightly. Amelia wasn't fooled. Helen was waiting anxiously for her answer.

What could she say? He's the man I'd least like to be marooned with on a desert island? He's the epitome of everything I despise and I hope I never see him again? He's an out-of-work loner with no apparent social skills, and if that wasn't enough, he's awfully full of himself?

She cleared her throat. "Granny, I'm sure Mr. Wolf is a good neighbor, and you're fortunate to have him close by. As for me, I'm almost engaged to a wonderful man. His name is Jeff Mason. I think you'd like him. We have a lot in common. He's very successful."

"You'll have to forgive me," Helen said, rubbing her palms briskly together. "I'm not up to date on the latest terms. What does 'almost engaged' mean, exactly?"

"Well, in this case, it means he's asked me, but I haven't said yes yet."

"Why not?"

Why not? That was a good question. What was she waiting for? Lightning to strike? Bells to ring? A prince to come riding up and sweep her away? She wasn't naive enough to believe life was like that. "I…I'm not sure."

"If you're not sure, that's a good reason to say no."

"I'll have to decide when I get back. What was it you used to say— 'Absence makes the heart grow fonder'?"

"For somebody else," her grandmother added with a wink.

Amelia went to the window and looked out. There was a ladder leaning against the apple tree. There was no vehicle and no obnoxious neighbor.

"Brian was here this morning," Granny said. "He was good enough to lend me his ladder so you can pick some apples for a pie. I told him to stay for coffee, but he had to run off to do some errands in town."

"Too bad," Amelia murmured. "Tell me more about him." Maybe if Helen got it off her chest, she'd leave Amelia alone.

"He's a wonderful man," Helen enthused, her eyes glowing. "So kind and generous. He knows I'm not supposed to go up and down stairs until my hip heals, so he's promised to make a ramp for me so I can get outside to the garden. Isn't that sweet?"

"Very sweet," Amelia agreed. "But wouldn't that be a lot of work, and make a lot of noise and saw-dust? I mean, you're supposed to be resting or nap-ping or whatever, and I thought I might do a little work while I'm here." After all, wouldn't that mean the man would be outside the house, pounding and hammering, just when she was trying to work up-stairs? "Sweet, but not necessary. I can help you down the stairs when you want to go."

"Oh, I hadn't thought about that. It was so sweet of him to offer, I didn't want to hurt his feelings, not after what he's been through."

"What has he been through?"

"That's not for me to say. If he wants you to know his background, he'll tell you. I'm sure he will. You just have to be patient."

Patient? As if she really wanted to know his back-ground or what he'd been through! "I will," Amelia said. "I promise not to ask him one single question about his past, or about anything at all. Don't worry about the ramp. I'll speak to him about it. You know, when I asked him what he did, I was just being polite. Believe me, it doesn't matter to me at all. I really don't care."

"I think you're protesting a little too much," Helen said with a wink. "Whatever you say, you must admit he's a good-looking man."

"I really didn't notice," Amelia said breezily.

"Not notice? Come now, Amelia, you're a red-blooded American woman in your prime. If I were your age…"

"What would you do, Granny, throw yourself at his feet?"

"I'd just be nice to him, that's all," Helen said primly. "These things take time."

"I only have a week or two, and by the way, I *was* nice to him," Amelia said.

"*Very* nice."

"All right," Amelia said reluctantly. "I'll be *very* nice to him. If I see him again, which I doubt. I think he's already brought the ladder by, so chances are I won't be running into Brian again. I'm sure he's just as uninterested in me as I am in him. I have the feeling he's not looking for company. Perhaps that's the real reason we really didn't hit it off."

"You didn't?" Granny's eyes widened in surprise. "I thought you were getting along famously."

"Granny, he's just not my type."

"Not your type? The type with big, broad shoulders and a brilliant mind, a granite jaw and a face like a movie star is not your type?"

Amelia sighed. She didn't want to talk with Granny about men in general, or any one man in particular. Granny had always been a little too perceptive.

"What is your type, then?" Granny asked.

Amelia sighed again. How had she gotten into this conversation? "Someone who shares my interests, who's geographically desirable and who—"

"By that you mean someone who lives in the city."

"Well, yes," Amelia said. "Since that's where I live. Not that I don't love it here, but…"

"There's nothing to do—is that what you were going to say?"

"There's no work to do, Granny. And work is what I do. I have to earn a living, you know."

"Of course I do," Granny said. "And I'm very proud of you." Granny gave her a warm smile, and the conversation was over. But Amelia couldn't get it out of her mind. What more could she say to convince the dear lady that her matchmaking was not going to work?

Instead of saying anything, Amelia drew a stick figure on her shopping list. Then she drew a dog next to the figure and a ladder in the figure's hands. Then she crossed it out with thick double lines, a little more forcefully than she needed to. "I'd better get going to the store. Anything else?"

"The pharmacy. Here's the prescription for my pain pills." Granny looked at the grandfather clock in the corner. "Go there first, because the pharmacist is only there from ten to twelve." Helen added a few more items to her list, and Amelia grabbed a sweatshirt and drove to the nearby town of Pine Mountain. She parked and strolled down Main Street, noticing that not much had changed since the last time she'd been there—the diner, with its long counter; the small grocery store and the old-fashioned drugstore with the soda fountain at the front and the pharmacy at the rear. She'd just handed the pharmacist the prescription when she heard a voice from behind her.

"Well, if it isn't Little Red Riding Hood."

She wished she hadn't worn the red hooded sweatshirt she'd found in the upstairs closet, but it was cool out this morning, and now it was too late to take it off. She clamped her jaw shut to keep from saying something rude. She turned her head slightly, but not far enough to see his so-called movie-star face or his granite jaw.

"What are you doing here?" she asked, barely able to keep the annoyance out of her voice.

"Getting some medicine for your grandmother." He held up a small, white prescription, just like the one Amelia had.

"That's what I'm doing. I don't know why she asked you… Oh, yes I do. Look, I'm sorry about this. She's got this idea that you and I… Never mind." Amelia was babbling. She couldn't stop. All she could think of was him standing beneath her window this morning looking right through her nightgown. "Give me your prescription, and I'll get them both filled," she said.

"No, you won't," Brian said. "I said I'd pick up the pills and I will. You can be on your way now."

"It doesn't make sense," Amelia said. "It's out of your way, and I'm going straight back home."

"All right," he said. "You can do it. I have to go to the hardware store next."

"So do I. Don't you see what she's up to?" Amelia rested her hands on her hips. "I adore her, but honestly, the woman is unbelievable. When she gets something in her head, there's no stopping her. I don't know what she thought would happen when we ran into each other here."

"Don't you?" Brian asked. "At the very least, she thought we'd have to exchange polite greetings and maybe stop for coffee at the diner, and at the most, I'd ravish you in the front seat of my truck."

He was amused to see Amelia's eyes flash and her face turn red at his last remark. He remembered that she'd blushed once last night. So she wasn't made of stone, after all. He wondered what it would take to get a real reaction out of her. He had no doubt that she'd never been ravished in the front seat of a truck, nor did she find the idea the least bit appealing. As for him, he hadn't wanted to ravish anyone for many months, and he certainly wouldn't start with an up-tight, out-of-place city girl.

"Since none of those things is going to happen," she said, blinking rapidly, "we'll split up, and I'll do the hardware shopping. Just give me your list."

"Hardware is man's work," he said. He hoped she'd realize he was joking. He was as much a fem-inist as any guy. But she didn't laugh or even smile. "Why don't you run along," he suggested. "Go home and pick apples, and make your famous apple pie I've been hearing so much about."

"She told you I made a famous apple pie?"

"It made my mouth water," he said. That much was true. He had a weakness for homemade pie dat-ing back to childhood. It certainly wasn't anything his ex-wife had ever made.

"Well, too bad. I'm not apple picking right now. I'm going to the hardware store." She turned on her heel and headed out the door. She looked deflated after coming all the way to town, then realizing it was for nothing. He almost felt sorry for her. He put the prescription on the counter, went out to the street and caught up with her.

"Amelia," he said. "Wait. If you really want to go

to the hardware store, go ahead. Here's my list." He stuck it in her hand.

She looked startled. Maybe it was because he'd called her by her name. It felt strange, rolling off his tongue. It was actually a nice name, feminine and musical and a little old-fashioned. But it didn't suit her at all.

"Thanks," she said. She glanced down at the list. "What's silicone caulk?"

"It's a sealant to stop leaks. Comes in a tube. I better take care of this stuff. Give me back the list." He reached for it.

"No." She crumpled it in her fist.

This was getting ridiculous. "You go on to the hardware store," he said. "That way, you can feel useful. And I'll meet you there to make sure you've gotten the right things."

"I have no need to *feel* useful," she snapped. "I *am* useful. I am not a stranger to hardware stores. The clerks there are usually helpful, so I'll be able to manage quite well on my own. Thank you, anyway." She shrugged out of the sweatshirt and tied it around her waist, then she spun around on her heel again and marched purposefully down the street.

He stood watching her for a long moment, her hips swaying in her tight jeans and her hair shining like a beacon in the sunlight on Main Street. A carpenter on scaffolding gawked at her, and two teenage boys on skateboards whistled. Yes, she was just what the town needed—a redheaded spitfire with a body that didn't quit and a mind of her own. Good thing she was leaving in a week or two, or every man between seventeen and seventy would be ogling her, unaware of her fiery temper. That shouldn't bother him, but it did. A little.

Chapter Three

Amelia hurriedly completed the hardware shopping before he could come by and check up on her. With her arms full of supplies, she passed a pickup truck on the street with a dog in the passenger seat. When the dog saw her, he barked enthusiastically and pressed his nose against the glass.

She looked around. Brian Wolf was nowhere in sight. She went up to the truck window.

"Hello, dog," she said. She'd forgotten his name. Actually, she'd never spoken to a dog before in her life. But he seemed pleased that she'd come to see him. She shifted the bags in her arms and reached in through the half-open window to rub the dog's nose with her knuckles. He made a soft whinnying sound.

Too bad the dog's owner didn't have half the charm of his dog.

On the way to her car she passed the diner. When she glanced in, she saw Brian Wolf sitting on a stool at the counter with a plate in front of him. As she passed, he turned his head and looked at her. She walked faster, pretending she hadn't seen him, rushing by before he could offer to buy her a cup of coffee or ravish her in the front seat of his truck. But she had seen him, and he knew it. She just hoped he hadn't seen her talk to his dog. He'd think she was some kind of nutcase.

"You just missed him," her grandmother said when she walked in the door of the cottage.

Amelia didn't bother to ask who she'd just missed. She saw the pills on the kitchen table. "How did that happen? I just saw him in town," she said.

"Really?" Granny said.

Amelia decided to accept her grandmother's wide-eyed, innocent look as bona fide. "We divided up the errands. It worked out better that way."

"I hope it wasn't too much trouble."

"Not at all," Amelia said, determined not to get into the same old discussion with her grandmother. "Now let me fix your lunch."

"I already had a sandwich. I made one for you, too."

"You should stay off your feet."

"It only took a few minutes."

Amelia looked around the kitchen. There was not only a sandwich on the counter, but a pot of soup on the stove, and the breakfast dishes had been washed. Amelia was just going to admonish her grandmother when Granny spoke up.

"Now, Amelia, I can't just sit on the couch all day. I'll go quite crazy with boredom. It can't hurt for me to do a few things around the house. Which reminds me—Brian has one of those exercise balls that you squeeze to increase the strength in your hands. He says it's just what I need. I wonder if you'd mind picking it up at his house. It's really just a short walk through the woods."

Amelia sighed. Would she never quit? "Of course." She didn't ask why her neighbor couldn't bring it over. "I'll go right now."

"Have your lunch first," Helen said. "There's plenty of time. Time to make an apple pie, too."

Amelia looked at her watch. It was after noon and she hadn't accomplished a thing. She thought longingly of her makeshift office upstairs and all the work she could be doing. And yet, with the sun shining and the air cool and fresh, the woods beckoned to her. Even if it meant a brief meeting with the neighbor. She'd get to her work this afternoon after she made the apple pie she was supposedly so good at.

"Just one thing, Granny. Your friend Brian? You're right, with his granite jaw and chiseled grin or grizzled chin or whatever else you said, I admit he's a very attractive man, but he's really not the right man for me. I'm sure he won't have any trouble finding someone more, uh, suitable for him. Unless he's not looking, of course."

"I'm afraid that is the problem," said Granny, a frown wrinkling her brow. "He thinks he doesn't need anyone."

"Then maybe we should take him at his word. Not everyone needs your help matchmaking for them."

"Not everyone, no."

"Just me and your friend, is that right?"

Granny pressed her lips together as if she were afraid of saying something that would put Amelia off. But it was clear she thought she knew what was best for everyone. It was just as clear to Amelia there was no way to stop her grandmother from doing what she was set on.

"If you knew Brian as I do, you'd understand," Granny said at last. "You don't know what happened to him."

"No, I don't." Amelia certainly didn't intend to find out, either. And yet... And yet, Granny had piqued her curiosity. "Since I won't have time to get to know him, why don't you fill me in on his story. Or are you sworn to secrecy?"

"All I can say is that something very terrible and tragic happened to him about a year ago. It's no surprise that he hasn't gotten over it, but I just wish I could help him. What he's done is seal himself away in his house. He hardly ever goes to town, which is why I'm so grateful to him for making the effort today. I'm really his only friend around here, which is not right. He needs people his own age who are interested in him and what he does. He needs to get back to doing what he's good at."

"Which is?" Amelia blurted, then caught herself. It was *none* of her business.

"You'll just have to ask him, dear."

Amelia nodded, but she had no intention of asking Brian Wolf anything except to hand over the exercise ball, if, indeed, it really existed and wasn't just another of Granny's excuses to get them together.

So instead of going up to her room and working on a software glitch, Amelia changed into shorts and knotted a men's tailored, white cotton shirt at her waist and went on her way through the woods to Brian Wolf's house. Before she left, her grandmother took a look at her outfit and frowned.

"Is that what you're wearing?" she asked.

Amelia hid a smile. "That's it," she said brightly.

"Didn't you bring a skirt or a sundress?" Granny asked.

"Yes, but I'm in the country now and I'm going for a walk in the woods. It's not as if I'm going to a square dance, is it? I can't tell you what a relief it is not to have to dress up anymore. I've unpacked my suitcase and hung my suit and high heels in the back of the closet up there. I actually found this old shirt in a drawer upstairs. I'm not sure where it came from…if you're saving it for something special…?"

"I think I was saving it for the Goodwill," her grandmother said drily. "I was just wondering if you'd want to wear something more…feminine."

"Nope," Amelia said cheerfully.

"And your hair…" Granny said. "That's not how you usually wear it."

Amelia brushed her bangs out of her eyes. She'd pulled her long hair into a knot at the nape of her neck. "No, you're right. For as long as I'm here, I'm going natural. I won't have to check in with my stylist, for once."

"No makeup?"

"Right again."

Granny sighed, then decided to put the best face on it. "Well, you look very…clean."

"Good." Amelia kissed Granny on the forehead. If her nature-girl look didn't convince Granny she wasn't looking for Mr. Right, it ought to at least convince her neighbor. Maybe he'd relax and stop treating her like an intruder and just accept her for what she was—an outsider, yes, but one with no motive other than to help her grandmother.

Blue jays swooped overhead and squirrels scampered up the tall oak trees along the path. The sun on her bare legs made her feel like skipping, which she hadn't done in years. Pine needles crunched under the soles of her running shoes. Somewhere in the distance she heard the sound of someone splitting wood. She'd only left the city yesterday, but already she felt like she was in another world. So why not relax and stop worrying about her work? Truthfully, she hadn't thought about the office and the work she'd brought home for hours.

"Well," Brian said to his dog, setting his ax down and wiping the sweat off his face. "I don't have to ask what you think of her. I saw how you behaved when she stopped to pet you at the truck. It's blatantly obvious you've fallen for her. What's wrong with you? Can't you see she's just like Natalie? The same city clothes, attitude and personality. I can understand why you like Helen. Don't think I haven't seen her sneak you those doggy treats. But Amelia? I don't get it. What is it? What do you see in her?"

His dog looked at him, his face cocked to one side.

"Never mind. It doesn't matter. It's the hair, isn't it? Okay, I admit it's an unusual color. It catches the eye. But there's more to women than their hair. If you don't know that by now… At least admit she doesn't belong here. Didn't you see what she was wearing yesterday? Don't be fooled by the jeans and the sweatshirt today. After one week, she'll be gone, with her fancy shoes and her suit and her red hair, and we'll be alone again, which is what we want. Which is why we're here. Which is why we put up the sign, isn't it? Well, isn't it?

"It was working pretty well, I thought. Until yesterday. Until *she* comes barging in here. If it weren't for her grandmother…

"Don't give me that look. I go over there only to see Helen. To help her out. So I offered to do her errands and bring some firewood. Who else is going to do it?

"You don't think I've forgotten why I've sworn off women, do you? You don't think I'll ever forget, do you? Because I won't. And don't tell me it's time to rejoin the human race. I've had enough of humans, that's why I have you.

"You're everything women are not. You're loyal, friendly and faithful." He scratched the dog under his chin. "They, on the other hand, are ambitious, cold and determined. Isn't it obvious she fits the image? And I'm having no part of it, no matter how hard our dear friend Helen tries. I'm never going through that again, and you know why…."

"Ahem."

There was nothing wrong with talking to your dog, Brian assured himself, but it was slightly embarrassing when you were caught in the act.

"What good are you?" he muttered as his neigh-

bor's granddaughter walked through the gate and his
dog didn't even bark. Dante approached her with
such enthusiasm and naked adoration that Brian just
stood there, shaking his head. The dog just didn't listen. The dog didn't think. The dog relied on instinct.
He, on the other hand, had submerged his instincts.
Instincts only got you into trouble.

"I wasn't expecting anyone," he explained, grabbing his shirt and throwing it on.

"Why doesn't that surprise me? Granny told me
you'd offered her some kind of exercise ball to
strengthen her grip. But you didn't, did you? I should
have known it was a setup. Never mind." She turned
to leave. Then she turned around and eyed him curi-
ously. "Tell me, does your dog understand what
you're saying?"

"Yes, he does," Brian said firmly. "And the best
thing? Dante never talks back. No smart answers. He
just listens."

"An admirable trait," she agreed. "And an admirable name. Maybe that's what I need—a dog. Only,
I can't have one in my apartment. Well, goodbye."

"Wait a minute," he said. "As long as you're here,
you could take your grandmother the electric can
opener I fixed for her a while ago. It's in the barn.
I'll be right back." He didn't invite her to come with
him. He didn't even know why he'd remembered
about the can opener. But here she was, dressed in

a shirt that gave him a tantalizing glimpse of the smooth skin at her waist and short shorts that showed off her long, long legs, with her hair in some kind of knot behind her head. The one thing she had going for her, that sensational hair, he couldn't see much of because of how she'd tied it back. It just made him want to yank off the band that held her hair in place and let the sun shine on it. Maybe let it fall through his fingers. No, no. What was he thinking?

Amelia obviously hadn't gotten the message—wait for me here—because she followed him and his dog around the back of the house to his converted barn.

"What do you need a barn for?" she asked.

"What does anyone need a barn for?" he asked, pausing at the wide double doors to look into her dark brown eyes. Anything to avoid gazing at that shirt and imagining how she'd look if it came unbuttoned, which it wouldn't—not without an act of nature like a bolt of lightning or a flash flood. "It's a workshop and a storage area," he said brusquely.

"A workshop," she repeated. "I thought you didn't do any work."

"I don't, but I did."

"Oh."

He didn't want her to see his shop. He didn't want her to see his house, either. He wanted to be left alone. He knew how women operated. Give them an inch and they took a mile. Now he was sorry he'd ever mentioned the can opener.

"Don't worry," she said. "I'm not coming in. I wouldn't dream of violating your privacy. I'll just wait out here."

She was perceptive, he'd give her that. She knew he didn't want her around. He only hoped she wasn't perceptive enough to know that she affected him where he least wanted to be affected. In the gut. Seeing her this morning in her window, in that seethrough nightgown, had caused him a near meltdown. Then he'd met her in the drugstore, and now she'd arrived unexpectedly on his land in those short shorts that showed off her long, smooth legs and that maddening white shirt that set his imagination going at warp speed.

He ought to be glad she wasn't in some skimpy halter top. Because it was warming up today, and he himself had been shirtless. Sure, he resented her citygirl black suit, but still... That didn't mean he wanted to see her stripped down and going country. It was all so phony. And now she'd followed him to the door of the barn. Watching her pet his dog made him feel as if the walls of his defenses were crumbling. That couldn't be. Not after he'd spent all this time constructing them.

He squared his shoulders. "I'll be right out," he said, and closed the barn doors after him and Dante.

* * *

Amelia stared at the closed doors. She couldn't believe he'd closed them in her face. She didn't really think he'd invite her in, but still… She felt hurt and left out. She told herself it was just a barn, and it was *his* barn, but still… She couldn't help wondering what was in there that he didn't want her to see. Curiosity—it got the better of her instinct and manners.

She walked around to the side of the rough-hewn building. There was a window, too high for her to look in. She dragged a step ladder over and stepped up on it. By standing on tiptoe she could see into a huge space filled with such an amazing sight, she almost fell off the ladder. Her mouth flew open as she gazed in surprise through the cobwebs into the cavernous barn. So this was his secret. So this was what he was hiding. But why? She got off the ladder and stood at the double barn door, just where he'd left her, trying to look innocent.

"Here you are," he said. He closed the door behind him and handed her a carton. If she asked him now, he'd know she'd peeked. If she said nothing, she might not get another chance.

"Well," she said, stalling for time while she thought up an appropriate way to broach the subject. "Granny will be happy to get her can opener, but are you sure you don't have an exercise ball?"

"Don't think so. But why couldn't she use any

rubber ball? I've got a supply I use to throw for Dante to chase. Don't worry—they're fresh, never even been chewed or slobbered on."

"Thanks."

This time, he headed for his house and she followed close behind. If he wouldn't invite her in to the barn, maybe the house wasn't off-limits. She had a feeling there might be a clue to the man's secret inside.

But there wasn't. He hesitated a moment, then held the front door open for her, and when she looked around, she was impressed by his taste—wide-plank floors with handwoven Native American rugs; deep, wide leather chairs; huge windows with views of the distant mountains. But no photographs on the wall, no incriminating journals or papers on the slab of polished redwood that served as a rustic coffee table.

"Nice house," she said.

"I like it. But it's not everybody's taste."

"What do you mean? It's beautiful."

"It's isolated. Far from town. Not many neighbors."

"I assume that's what you like about it."

"That's right." He handed her a pink rubber ball. Then he glanced at the door, obviously a hint. She chose to ignore it. She knew she ought to leave. She knew he didn't want her here. He didn't want anyone here. But she couldn't leave without making an effort to find out why. She couldn't help it. She was curious. Anyone would be after seeing what she'd seen.

"I wonder," she said, fanning her face. "Could I have a glass of water before I start back?"

"What? Oh, sure. My hospitality skills need work, which you may have noticed. I'm sorry, it's a warm afternoon and you look…hot." Now why had he said that? She shot him a quick look to see how he'd meant it, and he continued as smoothly as he could. "What I mean is…I'm not much of a host."

"Well, I'm not much of a guest. First I come under false pretenses, then I spy on you."

He didn't deny it. "I'll be back in a minute." She nodded and sat down in one of his leather chairs. He looked surprised, probably afraid she was planning on staying for a while. She wasn't. She was just waiting, just observing. She was curious about him. There was nothing wrong with that, was there? The only thing was that the more she found out, the more she wanted to know.

As soon as he left the room, she stood up and prowled around the spacious room. Against the wall, there was a small table with a basket overflowing with envelopes and paper. Half-opened mail, if she wasn't mistaken. She had no intention of reading it. But when she got close, she saw a large legal-size envelope with the return address of the hands-on, prestigious children's museum in San Francisco.

When he returned, she was back in her chair. "Thanks," she said, taking the tall glass of ice water from his hands. She had made up her mind to ask her question. After all, what was the worst he could do? Refuse to answer? Throw her out?

He raised his eyebrows at the sight of her slowly drinking her water, no doubt wondering if she was ever going to leave. When she'd drained her glass and handed it back to him, his hand brushed hers, and once again she felt her pulse speed up. His gaze locked with hers and she knew he'd felt it, too. Felt it, but didn't like it any better than she did. He took a step backward and stared at her with narrowed eyes.

She took a deep breath. "You'll think I'm a terrible snoop," she said. "But I couldn't help it. I looked into your barn from the window."

"Couldn't help it? What are you, some kind of detective? What were you looking for?"

"Nothing…nothing. I'm sorry. If you weren't so darned secretive, I wouldn't have looked." She got up and rocked back on the heels of her running shoes. She should leave, and leave now. But if she didn't ask now, she might never get another chance. She took a deep breath.

"I…uh… What is all that stuff?"

"That stuff, as you call it, is my life's work. Or was, until…" He didn't finish his sentence. He folded his arms across his chest, his forehead furrowed.

She waited. The silence grew and grew. He gazed out the window, as if he'd forgotten she was there, and she didn't know how to proceed. She shifted from one foot to the other. She could leave now and save them both any further embarrassment, or she could press on.

"They… It looked like a kind of toyland."

"You're very observant."

"But who? What? How?"

"Who?" he repeated. "Me. I made them. What? They're toys, of course. And how? That's a long story I don't want to bore you with. I've already taken too much of your time."

"But what about…?" What about that letter in his unopened mail pile from the Children's Toy Museum? What was that about? Were his toys museum quality? She bit her lip. No, she couldn't say anything more. He'd made his point. She'd taken too much of *his* time. What could she do when he opened the front door but leave? He was sorry she'd come. Sorrier she'd spied on him. She bit her lip to keep from asking the questions that burbled forth in her brain: Why keep the toys locked up in a barn? Why hide them, and yourself, from the world? Who and what was he hiding from? Had he designed them, made them, made money on them?

She kept the questions to herself for the moment, and with a polite smile, she took herself and the boxed can opener and the squishy pink rubber ball and headed down the path to Granny's. The sight of rusty bicycles, dusty hoops, wheels and spikes, twisted wires and huge machine tools was dancing in her brain. Along with that letter.

But the sight she really couldn't get out of her mind was the man without his shirt. She'd only had a momentary glance at the smooth muscles of his chest covered with a fine dusting of dark hair, his bare arms raised above his head before he put his shirt on, his arm muscles flexed, but it was an image she couldn't shake. It was the body of a man who did physical work, not like the guys at her health club. No getting around it, the man was gorgeous. Why he hadn't been taken by some woman by now was beyond her. Unless it was his prickly personality. No amount of good looks would balance that. Some women might consider him a challenge. Not her. She had enough challenges in her life without a man like Brian Wolf.

Chapter Four

When she got back, Amelia refrained from telling Granny she was on to her well-meaning tricks. She simply gave Helen her new ball and repaired can opener and helped her down the steps into the garden, where she sat on a lounge chair under the apple tree with her knitting.

"You took your time," Granny observed, that knowing twinkle in her eye.

"Who, me?" Amelia asked innocently.

"Yes, you. You must have made a hit with our Brian."

Amelia shook her head. "'Fraid not," she said. "The only reason he tolerates me is because I'm related to you. I got your ball and your can opener, and

I got a drink of water for myself and that was it." She didn't say anything about the toys. Granny would only say "He'll tell you when you get to know him better, and when he wants you to know," and that would be never. Amelia had her own ways of digging out facts, and she lost no time taking the steps to the tiny bedroom and her computer.

She tried to raise the windows to let the fresh air in, but the they were stuck shut, and the heat under the eaves was oppressive. In a few minutes, the perspiration was dripping down her temples, but she had a few answers. A few answers but even more questions.

"Granny, do you have a chisel or a hammer? I need to pry open those windows in the bedroom."

"Oh, dear, it's warmed up this afternoon and the heat rises. The windows sometimes get stuck. I'll just give Brian a call. He has all the tools for the job."

"No, don't do that. I'll get what I need at the hardware store and then I can do it."

"I don't mean to interfere, Amelia, but it doesn't hurt to be a little helpless now and then. Men like to take charge. In my day—"

"Don't tell me you let Grandfather take charge. Who painted those windows year after year? Who put up the screens, and who even got her fingers dirty laying the flagstones in the driveway? Not Grandpa. He was upstairs, writing his memoirs."

Granny chuckled. "All right, I admit it, but the important thing is he thought he was in charge."

"So you tricked him."

"Maybe. Maybe not. I call it a division of labor. Surely that's not out-of-date, too."

"That's what I mean," Amelia said agreeably. "We'll just borrow the tools from your neighbor, because I feel like we've already intruded enough." Enough? She'd intruded way too much. "I have the distinct feeling he doesn't want to be disturbed."

"He doesn't think he does, but really, you're good for him. Already, I see a change in him. For the better."

Amelia could only imagine what he'd been like before if he was better now. She looked around the garden at the overgrown strawberry patch and at the apple tree heavy with yellow-green Golden Delicious apples. Yes, she should go up and get busy working, but it was so hot up there, and so nice down here with the breeze rustling the leaves and the scent of ripe apples filling the air. And there were all those apples hanging there, just begging to be picked. So she did. She hauled the ladder to the tree, and under the watchful eye of her grandmother, who made suggestions from where she sat while beaming her approval, Amelia soon had a basket full of apples.

Back in the kitchen, Amelia didn't think she'd remember how to make her grandmother's crust, but it all came back to her, in the same way as riding a bicycle did. Bicycle... That reminded her of Brian Wolf, and the information she'd gotten about him off the Internet. As she rolled her crust, she once again wondered what the "brilliant inventor of children's toys and developer of performance bikes" was up to now. Was it really "nothing"? And if so, why? What was the tragedy that had put a stop to his life's work? She'd just slipped the pie into the oven when her cell phone rang. She ran up the stairs and came clattering back down while she talked.

"Fine, I'm just fine," she told Jeff as she fanned herself with her hand, opened the screen door and went out onto the front porch to cool off—and talk out of range of Granny's sharp ears in the orchard.

"Getting any work done?" he asked.

"Not really. Unless you count making a pie."

"A pie? You're making a pie?" He sounded as surprised as if she'd said she was spinning gold out of yarn. "What about all the things you were working on at the office?"

Amelia frowned. She didn't want to be reminded of the work that waited for her upstairs. She didn't need anyone to urge her to work harder.

"This is Saturday." She realized as soon as she'd said it that she often worked on Saturday, and that he knew it. "I'm taking the weekend off. I'll get to it on Monday. Right now the windows are painted shut and it's hot and—"

"Turn on the air-conditioning," he said.

Amelia took a deep breath. Had Jeff ever been in the country? Had he ever been in a house or a building without air-conditioning?

"Right," she said, unwilling to explain it all to him. "How's everything back there?"

"Great. Everyone's going out tonight to celebrate Marty and Joe's engagement."

"That's right. Sorry I can't make it. Give them my best, and let them know I'm out of town, will you?"

"Sure. You know what they want to know—when is it our turn? When will they celebrate our engagement?"

"Oh…well…" He would have to start in, just when she was out of town and feeling disconnected. "We'll talk about it when I get back."

"When will that be?"

"I don't know. That depends on how Granny does."

"I don't understand why you have to take care of her. Can't you hire someone, a health-care professional, to do the job?"

"Maybe, but it's not the same. I'm family."

There was a long silence while Jeff digested this, and she couldn't think of anything else to say. Then Jeff told her about a run-in he'd had with his boss, and she had to listen while he went into the details of the argument, as the smell of apples and cinnamon came wafting out the door, lulling her into a kind of daze, reminding her of just how far away she was from Jeff, both geographically and emotionally.

"I have to go now, Jeff."

"You don't sound like yourself, Amelia. We'll talk when you get back. I have something to ask you, and this time I want an answer."

She *knew* what he wanted to ask her and she didn't *have* an answer, so she said goodbye abruptly and hung up.

She'd just taken the pie out of the oven and was admiring her work on the fluted crust when Brian Wolf appeared in the doorway, tall, dark and disturbingly good-looking in cargo pants and a rumpled T-shirt. Granny was right, of course. He was attractive. But although that was no reason to be so flustered, she almost dropped the pie.

"Don't you ever knock?" she asked, setting the pie on Granny's worn pine hutch to cool.

"You're asking *me?*" he said, his eyebrows raised in surprise.

"All right, all right. I came to your house unannounced, without knocking. Did you have a hot and heavy pie in your hands?"

"Worse. I had an ax. I could have chopped my toes off."

She let her gaze travel down his legs to his feet. "I see they're still intact."

"I see you've been baking." He leaned forward

and wiped a smudge of flour from her nose with his thumb, and she drew in a sharp intake of breath. What was wrong with her? A simple gesture had her shaking inside. "Actually, I smelled it."

"All the way at your house?" she asked, leaning back against the kitchen counter. "I find that hard to believe."

"When the wind is right, smells carry." He inhaled deeply. "Sounds, too."

"And sights. Was that you burning the midnight oil last night?" she asked.

"Guilty as charged."

"I thought country folk went to bed with the chickens."

"Some of us have insomnia. That's not your problem. Your lights were out at ten."

"You were spying on me?" she asked.

"Force of habit. I keep an eye on your grandmother."

"I'm here now. You can relax," she said.

Brian nodded. Relax. Easy for her to say. He hadn't relaxed since that fateful day over a year ago, when Natalie had run off and hadn't come back. There was a long silence. The room was filled with heat from the oven and the rich smell of hot apples and flaky brown crust. Amelia looked as uncomfortable as he felt. Her face was flushed, her glorious red hair had come loose from the knot and curled in tendrils around her face. There was yet another smudge of flour on her cheek, and his fingers itched to brush it off. But the touch of her skin a few minutes ago had sent his temperature soaring, and it had nothing to do with the heat from the oven. So he tried to ignore the flour and her hair and the way her shirt had come unbuttoned at the neck to expose the valley between her breasts.

He searched his mind for something to say, something to lighten the atmosphere and to cut through the tension that was building. He couldn't tell her why he was here because he wasn't sure himself. Lately he was more comfortable at Helen's than he was in his own home. Why, he didn't know. He only knew he was restless. He'd started out from his house walking in the opposite direction, only to turn around, pick up his tool kit and head for Helen's cottage as if it were a magnet.

Yes, he'd smelled the pie baking, but not until he'd arrived on the front steps. Yes, he'd received a call from his neighbor about the windows. And yes, he'd seen the unmistakable twinkle in Helen's eyes when she greeted him, and knew what she was thinking. So he was here. It was better he come when the granddaughter wasn't around, but here he was. It didn't make any sense. But nothing had made sense for a long time.

"So," Amelia said at last. "You're here because you smelled apple pie?"

"No," he said more brusquely than he intended.

"I'm only here because your grandmother asked if I'd pry open the windows upstairs." He pointed to his tool kit he'd left at the door.

"I hope you don't think that was my idea, because there was no need for you to come. All I needed was the tools—a knife and a hammer—and I could do it myself. At least let me help."

He shrugged. It wasn't a two-man job, but if she needed to feel useful, as workaholics often did, who was he to stop her? In any case, she followed him up the narrow staircase and into the tiny bedroom. She'd only been there one night, and already her light, flowery scent filled the room. Her suitcase was open on the bed, and he noticed a tangle of silky underwear before she quickly closed it and shoved it under the bed. He bent over to open his tool kit and clear his head. So she smelled like wildflowers and wore silk underwear. So did most women. No big deal. No need to get excited. Relax, he told himself. Why was that so hard to do?

"How long is this going to go on?" she asked.

"What's that?" he asked, tapping a knife with a hammer against the window frame.

She leaned one shoulder against the woodwork. "Oh, come on. You know as well as I do that my grandmother is plotting to set us up. Can't you do something about it? Can't you discourage her?"

"What do you want me to say?" he asked, his face

turned toward the window so she wouldn't see that his mouth was turned up in a reluctant half smile.

"That you're not interested. That you're engaged to someone else. That you're gay or you're entering a monastery next week. I don't know. Use your imagination."

"Maybe I don't want to discourage her. Maybe I want her to throw us together. Maybe I saw your picture and I got fixated on you and I asked her to do it. It happens. Ever think of that?"

She snorted. "Oh, sure. That's why you have those signs up all over your house. That's why you've done your utmost to get rid of me. That's why you have a watchdog."

"Some watchdog," he muttered. "Okay, if you don't believe me, why don't *you* discourage her?"

"I've tried. I told her I was almost engaged."

"What does that mean?"

"That's what she said. I don't know." She sighed. Maybe she thought she owed him a better explanation, because she finally continued. "It means he's asked me but I haven't given him an answer."

"Why not?"

"That's none of your business."

"You started this conversation, not me." He tapped again, to break up the paint around the window, and the noise precluded her from coming up with any more answers—or any more questions, for that matter. When he jerked the window up, a breath of fresh air came into the room.

"That's great," she said. "Thank you."

"I'll get the other ones now."

"I'm not really helping, am I?"

"Not unless you consider those ridiculous suggestions being helpful."

"I'm just trying to save everyone a lot of trouble. Trying to keep Granny from getting her hopes up. She's an incurable romantic."

"I've noticed. But she's also a realist. You don't really think that she imagines you and I... No, she couldn't." He hit the knife with a little more force than was absolutely necessary.

"Why not? You're available. You're decent. She thinks you're reasonably attractive."

"Why, thank you, Ms. Amelia," he drawled.

"Don't thank *me*," she said huffily. "I'm just telling you what *she* thinks."

"Still, you have to watch out, or you might inflate my ego."

"And you're handy around the house."

"So what more do you want?" he asked from over his shoulder.

"I want someone with a job, for one thing," she said pointedly.

"Why, so you can stay home with the redheaded children?"

"I'm not planning on any redheads. They say it skips a generation."

"Does that mean you're planning on nonredheads?"

She straightened her shoulders. "The only plans I'm making are to brew some coffee in my espresso machine and serve pie outside in the garden. If you'd care to join me and Granny…"

"Count me in."

"I'm afraid I haven't been much help."

"You've stroked my ego. I can't ask for more than that."

"I didn't mean to," she said, but he noticed her lips curved in a reluctant grin anyway.

"You know what she says about you, don't you?" he asked.

"That I'm perfect?"

"And beautiful."

She blushed again. She wasn't beautiful, he thought, not in the usual sense. But there was something about her that made her easy to look at. It was the hair, of course, but something else, too. Before he could pinpoint what it was, she turned and went down the stairs. That blush, and the grin, along with her knotted shirt and shorts and lack of makeup, made her look not so much beautiful, but young and flirtatious. It made him feel young, younger than he had felt in years. Why was that? Was it her? Was it him? Was it them together? Could Helen be on to something? Of course not. That was ridiculous. Then why didn't he tell Helen he wasn't interested? Why didn't he make up an excuse, as Amelia had suggested?

He tapped a few more windows and thought about what she'd said. He wondered if she really wanted kids. He wondered if he should tell her what he did for a living, or rather, what he'd done and why he didn't do it anymore. She was curious about him. She thought he didn't work. She was right.

He had to admit he was curious about her. Curious about who the man was who'd proposed to her and why she hadn't said yes. About what kind of work she did. But he didn't want to ask her. That would send a message he didn't want to send. It would make her think he was interested in her. He wasn't. Not that way. He'd sworn off women. With good reason. He glanced at her computer and very casually hit the Enter button.

There in front of him was the Web page of his former company, with a list of the toys he'd invented and a description of each one. He stood there for a long moment, staring at the screen, feeling guilty, as if he were spying on her, when in reality she'd been spying him. Well, maybe *spying* was too strong a word. The information was there for anyone to look at. What was not there was why he'd stopped and why he hadn't done anything new for the past year. That much she didn't, and wouldn't, know. It was none of anyone's business. Of course, Helen knew, but he was confident she would keep his secrets. He put Amelia's computer to sleep and went downstairs.

The three of them ate pie together outside in the garden at the rough-edged redwood table that had seen its share of weather. Amelia had thrown a red-and-white-checkered tablecloth over it, and with the sunlight filtered through the trees and the taste of warm cinnamon and apples in his mouth, he felt strangely peaceful. He certainly didn't feel as if he wanted to bring up his past or let on that he knew she'd been looking him up. What did it matter?

When he finished his pie, he leaned back in his chair and gazed up at the sky.

"I must say, Amelia," Helen said, "you've outdone yourself. Don't you think so, Brian? Isn't this about the best apple pie you've ever had?"

"Granny…" Amelia said.

"Well, it is," Helen insisted.

"You're right," Brian said solemnly. "It is the best. No question."

"And now, if you two will excuse me… It's time for my nap." She braced her hands on the table.

"I'll help you." Brian jumped up. So did Amelia. With Amelia on one side and him on the other, they guided Helen up the steps into the living room and back onto the couch.

Helen closed her eyes and waved them away. "Go on, go have another cup of coffee. I'm tired. Let me be."

He exchanged a brief look with Amelia. She nodded and they went back outside. For a long moment, they stood on Helen's front porch.

"No more coffee for me," he said.

She nodded vigorously, as if she were more than anxious to get rid of him. "If you'll excuse me," she said, "I'm going up to do some work. I have to thank you for making the room workable."

"No problem. Call me anytime."

"I didn't call you the first time, and I can't guarantee that Granny won't call you again. In fact, I can pretty much guarantee that she will call you. Unless you do something about it."

"What, and spoil her fun? I wouldn't dream of it."

She shrugged. "Very well." She turned to go inside.

"Wait." He reached for her arm and turned her toward him. The thought of returning to his empty house or of taking a solitary walk through the woods didn't seem appealing. He wanted to sit under the trees and talk. She was so close, he could see a few freckles across her nose. Were those there before, or a result of the summer sunshine?

He brushed his fingers across her nose.

Her eyes widened. "What?" she asked, her voice just a little shaky. "More flour?"

"Freckles. You ought to stay out of the sun. With your fair skin—"

"Thanks for the warning," she said.

He dropped his hand. "I, uh, I owe you some kind of explanation."

"For what?"

"Being secretive. I don't know, maybe you're not interested in what I do, but—"

"I am. Of course I am. Sit down." She motioned toward the picnic table under the tree. "How about a glass of white wine? I brought some along in case Granny's cupboard was bare."

Before he could protest or change his mind, she'd gone back inside, and when she reappeared, she brought two wineglasses and a bottle of what he recognized as a very nice Chablis.

Amelia realized that what Brian was doing was out of character, and that if she didn't listen now she might never hear his story. For some reason, it was important to her. She'd read just enough on the Internet to pique her curiosity, and now she wanted to hear the whole story. But it was more than curiosity. How much more, she didn't know. Of course, he might not be willing to go *that* far and tell her everything, but maybe the wine would loosen his tongue.

Also, she'd noticed that he'd said "what I do," and not "what I used to do," which she took as a good sign. If Granny was right, it was time for him to get back to work.

If she, Amelia, the quintessential workaholic, could help him do that, she'd be remiss in not at least trying. That's what she told herself. But deep down, she could think of nothing she'd rather do on this warm summer afternoon, with the breeze brushing the leaves of the apple tree and the sunlight making patterns on the table-cloth, than sit across the table from this maddening, interesting, admittedly great-looking man, and talk.

"Who was it," Amelia said, pouring chilled wine into their glasses, "who said that *summer afternoon* were the two loveliest words in the English language?"

"I don't know," he said. "But I have to agree."

Amelia couldn't help but notice that the deep horizontal lines in Brian's forehead were gone. Maybe it was the shadow across his face, or the way the sun shone on his head, or maybe, just maybe, he was beginning to relax around her. Maybe he no longer considered her a nosy, predatory female with an agenda of her own. Or maybe it was just the day, the sun, the pie and this particular confluence of events would never happen again. All the more reason to sit down and see what happened.

It took a long time before he began talking. So long, in fact, she was afraid he had lost his nerve or his interest in talking about himself. At that point, she almost didn't care. It was so peaceful just sitting there, sipping wine, smelling the piney mountain air, with the sun on her shoulders. The silence that stretched between them wasn't awkward; it was downright comfortable.

"You saw the toys," he said at last.

"Well, yes," she said. "I saw them through the dusty window, but I didn't get a very good look. Really, this is none of my business…."

"I think you also got a look at them on the toy manufacturer's Web site."

"You didn't! You woke up my computer. So you saw that I'd looked you up. I make no apologies. I saw that you're famous. So that's the reason for the security and the dog and the signs?"

"Actually, hardly anyone comes looking for me anymore, so maybe I can take down the signs."

"That must be a relief."

"Yes…and no. Lately I've been wondering if I've done the right thing. Lately I've been, I don't know…" He ran his hand through his hair until it stood on end. "Bored."

"Tell me about the toys," she said eagerly, leaning across the table. "Why toys? Why not invent kitchen appliances? What made you invent toys?"

"Toys are fun. Toys are for kids. And kids… I thought by now I'd have kids, and when I did, I'd have someone to test them on. Someone to inspire me. What were your favorite toys?"

"I didn't have any."

"Toys or favorites? You must have had toys. Every kid has toys."

She shook her head. "Not me. My parents didn't believe in them. Oh, I had books and games. But they all had a point. They were all educational. But that's just me. Go on. I thought I saw a bicycle in the barn. What else?"

"What else? It would be easier to show you than describe them. The next time you come by…"

Amelia frowned. She had a sinking feeling he'd changed his mind and wasn't going to confide in her, after all. The next time she came by, he might have another excuse. If she wanted to know more about him and his toys, she had to make a move, and make it now. She didn't want to beg him. She didn't want to annoy him. But she wanted to know more and she'd do whatever it took to find out.

Chapter Five

But before she could do or say anything, she heard her cell phone ring. "I'll be right back," she said to Brian, and dashed into the house. It was Serena, her assistant.

"Sorry to bother you on your vacation, Amelia, but we've got an emergency."

"That's okay. It's not really a vacation. What's up?"

"One of our clients, Frantz and Fotre, is threatening to leave and use another company. I tried to call you yesterday but I couldn't get through."

"I know. My battery was dead." Amelia ran upstairs to her bedroom and sat on the edge of her bed. She flipped open her briefcase and tried to find the files Serena was talking about. Then she turned to her computer. When she had the information in front of her, she still had a hard time deciding on the right strategy. And she'd only been gone for a day! She forced herself to think, and she told her assistant she'd call the CEO of F and F on Monday. "Don't worry, I know what to say," she said. But did she? If she didn't, she would know by Monday. It served her right for drinking wine in the sun in the middle of the afternoon. She hoped she sounded reassuring, at least.

"Thanks for letting me know, Serena. Don't worry about it. I'll handle it."

She hung up, made a few notes, changed into a cool tank top and went back downstairs. Granny was sound asleep and Brian was in the same chair under the apple tree, his head tilted back, his eyes closed. She stood on the front step looking at him, noticing the way his dark hair angled across his forehead, just begging her to rearrange it back the way he usually wore it. She was amazed at how different he looked without the usual frown lines between his eyebrows. Maybe Granny was right, and she was crazy to dismiss him so easily. She shook her head. No, she wasn't. He had problems, even Granny admitted that. Amelia was no psychoanalyst. She couldn't force anyone back to work if they didn't want to go. She had a life, a job and a potential fiancé, if she wanted him. But in this setting, on this week, those things were just a blip on the computer screen of her life.

She cleared her throat. Brian opened his eyes suddenly and looked at her as if she'd appeared from nowhere.

"I can't believe I fell asleep," he said. "I never sleep during the day."

"Or at night, either, according to you. So it must be the sun and the wine," she suggested. "Granny's asleep, too."

"But she's just had surgery. I have no good excuse."

"Only that, besides the wine and the sun, you were up burning the midnight oil. What did you say you were doing?"

"I didn't." The frown lines were back. She'd pushed too hard. But that didn't stop her from pursuing her goal.

"About those toys... You said something about showing them to me."

"I did?"

"Never mind." She felt a surge of disappointment. If she didn't get to see them now, she might never have another chance. Not that it mattered. It was his life, his career, his toys. But it did matter. It mattered to her and it mattered to him. Or it should. He must have sensed her disappointment, because he gave her another chance.

"If you really want to see them..." he said, getting out of his chair.

"Yes, I do," she said quickly, before he could take

off without her. "I'll leave Granny a note, and she can call me on my cell phone if she needs me."

Before he could change his mind, or tell her they'd do it another day or she wouldn't be interested in his toys, she ran into the house, wrote the note and stuffed her phone into her back pocket.

They walked side by side down the narrow trail, their steps matching each other's. When his arm brushed hers, her skin radiated heat. With every touch, she felt her temperature rise. She felt as if every nerve ending was on alert, more sensitive than she believed possible. They didn't speak until Brian broke the silence.

"Who was that on the phone?"

What? Was the man really asking her a personal question? "It was my office with an emergency."

"On Saturday?"

"Some people work on Saturday," she said. "I used to." Had she really said she *used* to work on Saturday? As if she no longer worked on weekends? As if she wasn't going back to her real life in a matter of days, weeks at the most?

"So did I," he said. "But that's because it wasn't work. It was my life. I miss it," he added. She slanted a look in his direction. She couldn't believe he'd actually confided in her.

Brian changed the subject, as if he was embarrassed to have spoken from his heart. "Have you discovered the berry patch?" he asked.

"Blackberries? No. Where is it?"

"This way." He took her hand and pulled her through a thicket and out into a meadow edged by a giant mass of brambles.

"Wow, what a crop," she said, conscious of the warmth of his hand and strangely let down when he let go. "I think I used to come here as a kid. I'd forgotten about it." She reached between the thorny branches for a dark, juicy berry and popped it into her mouth. The sweet flavor exploded on her tongue, and she reached for another and another until her hands were stained.

His gaze shifted over her face, her shirt and her legs, and then back to her purple-stained lips.

"What's wrong?" she asked.

"You've got juice everywhere," he said.

She licked her lips. He leaned forward. If she didn't know better, if she didn't know he avoided contact with everyone, she would have thought he was going to kiss her. Even stranger, she wanted him to.

"Do you come here often?" she asked, wishing she didn't sound so breathless.

"Not often enough," he said, and he kissed her. She rocked back on her heels, shocked and surprised by the effect his kiss had. She'd kissed more than a few men in her time, but she'd never felt like this—

light-headed, shaky and yet strangely energized. From just one kiss. It must be the wine, the sun and the berries. It couldn't be this stranger, the one who avoided people like the plague. He was standing there, looking at her as if he was just as surprised as she was.

She felt so giddy, she laughed out loud. "Sorry, but you looked so surprised."

"I was," he said with a rueful grin. "I didn't mean to do that. Kiss you, I mean. But you've got that berry juice all over your lips and…" He shrugged. "I couldn't help it."

"You do, too. There are purple stains all over your mouth. I was afraid we'd stick together."

"I can think of worse ways to spend the afternoon." His mouth curved in a half smile, and his eyes gleamed.

"Why, Mr. Do Not Disturb, Beware of Dog, are you flirting with me?" she asked.

"I don't think so," he said, rubbing his chin thoughtfully.

She was flustered. Yes, this was what Granny had wanted to happen. But it was not what Amelia wanted. Now, what was it they'd been doing here? Oh, yes. She reached for another blackberry and got a thorn stuck in her finger.

"Ouch," she said.

He grabbed her hand. "Let me see that." He pulled

the thorn out, and a spot of blood dotted her thumb. "Let's go. I'll get you a bandage at my house."

"It's nothing. I'm fine."

"Brave lady."

She shook her head. "Flattery will get you nowhere."

"Not even another kiss?"

"Well…"

He put his hands on her shoulders, and this time he kissed her firmly and deliberately. The first kiss had been an experiment, a chance, a suggestion. This was nothing like that. This time he knew what he was doing, and so did she. She wrapped her arms around his neck and kissed him back. He tasted of the sweet-sour berries, and she couldn't seem to get enough of the taste, or of him. The sun beat down on her hair, the scent of dry, fragrant wild grass hung in the air and the buzzing of bees came from somewhere in the background. Her heart fluttered. He moaned deeply, and suddenly Amelia realized what they were doing, dropped her arms and broke the kiss.

"I shouldn't have done that," she said, knotting her hands together. What had she been thinking?

"No," he agreed calmly. "But I'm glad you did."

"Let's see," she said, wiping her forehead with her hand, "where were we?"

"On our way to my house."

"Your house? I should be getting back."

"I thought you wanted to see my stuff."

"Yes, but…" She was dizzy, disoriented. "What about Granny?"

"You've got your phone. And she's probably still asleep."

Neither one said that Granny would be more than pleased at the recent developments. But both of them thought it.

"How's your thumb?" he asked.

"My thumb?" What thumb? She looked at it as if it belonged to someone else. "Oh, fine."

They scrambled out of the brambles, went back to the trail and in minutes, they were at his house. Dante barked an enthusiastic greeting at the gate and followed them as they walked around to the barn. Amelia scratched the dog behind his ears while Brian opened the double doors. He hesitated for a long moment, as if he regretted his rash offer. As if he wished he'd let her go straight home from the berry patch.

"I don't know if these things will mean much to a girl who never had any toys," he said, one hand on the door handle.

"Maybe it's not too late," she said, peering inside at the shelves filled with plastic and metal parts, boxes and tools. "I think I deserve a second childhood."

That brought a half smile to his face. What an effort it was to coax one out of him, but she had to say—it was worth it. There were even small laugh lines at the corners of his eyes. Hard to believe, but once upon a time he'd laughed a lot. The question was—would he ever laugh again?

Now, more than ever, she wondered what had happened to him a year ago. Why had he stopped working? But now was not the time to ask. Not when he'd opened his barn to her. Which was really all she wanted. Just to see what was so special, so interesting in there that he had to guard it with warning signs and a watchdog. She certainly didn't want him to open his heart. Just his barn.

Brian realized it was too late to stop now. When she saw the contents, she might make polite remarks, she might not even bother. But they'd come this far and he was out of excuses. So he flipped on the light switches, and the whole barn was illuminated.

He watched her look around with an awed expression on her face. He watched her tiptoe past racks of toys as if she were in a museum. Then she started asking questions: "What's this?" "What do you do with that?" "How did you make this?"

She paused in front of one of his favorites.

"It's a pogo stick," he said. "Don't tell me you've never seen one before." She shook her head. He took it off the shelf and grabbed a helmet and a pair of knee pads. "I'll show you how it works."

He carried it outside into the sunlight. "Usually," he explained, "pogo sticks have springs here. This one is powered by air, so it has more kick."

Encouraged by the attentive look she gave him, he strapped on the knee pads and buckled the helmet under his chin. Then he bounced up and down on the gravel driveway. She clapped her hands and laughed out loud. He grinned at her and got off.

"Can I try?" she asked.

"Sure." He put the knee pads on for her, his fingers grazing the smooth skin on her long legs, then he snapped her helmet in place, tracing a line along the curve of her chin with his fingers. "In case you fall," he explained. But right now, he felt like he was the one in danger of falling. This afternoon was turning out to be a mind-boggling experience. He was afraid he was going to regret it, but right now, he wanted to see her on his pogo stick. For a girl who'd had no toys, it ought to be interesting.

"In case I fall? I will fall. I've never done this before."

She did fall, but she got up and tried again and again. She bounced, she laughed, she bit her lip and she jumped off. Finally, breathless and red-cheeked, she handed the pogo stick back to him. "That was great. I did okay, didn't I?"

"You did great. Are you sure you've never done it before?"

"Positive. My parents would never have let me."

"Too dangerous?"

"Too frivolous."

He could just imagine what she'd looked like as

a child, freckle-faced with red hair. He tucked a strand of her hair behind her ear and studied her red cheeks, her brown eyes and the tendrils of hair curling around her face. "Poor little girl."

"I had other things," she said defensively.

"Like books."

"And classes—music and French—and games. Games were all right, as long as they were educational." She glanced back at the barn. "What else have you got in there?"

"In-line skates that grow with the child, a play kitchen where the food turns color when it's done, kid-size toy cars with hand brakes and an adjustable bucket seat, a roller coaster six-and-a-half feet long that the kid has to construct, with real sounds, twists, turns and loops."

"You have some fantastic ideas."

"Unfortunately, most of what you've seen in there are just ideas—that's all they are. Oh, they're all patented, and I've made the prototypes, but only a few are in production at this time. About a year ago, I pulled most everything off the line. Nothing new has been tested since then. They're all just crude samples except for the pogo stick and the toy kitchen stove. I made those a few years ago, and they're still being sold. As you saw, everything else is coated with a layer of dust or rust. Everything is just sitting here, like me, waiting…."

"But why? Never mind. It's none of my business. You know, I've never been on a real roller coaster. My parents said they were dangerous and would make me sick."

"They were probably right. But if you want to try… There's a carnival over at Glenwood at the county fair. I was thinking of taking a day trip tomorrow to try it out. Research, you know."

"So you're still doing research. You *are* working."

"I'm only *thinking* about working. That's not the same. I've been thinking about it for a while."

"I'd like to go, but I couldn't leave Granny."

"Some other time." He was half disappointed, half relieved. It would take all day, and he knew spending another day with her was not a good idea. She put all kinds of ideas in his head. As if he was ready for some kind of a relationship with a woman, which he wasn't. Even if he was, it wouldn't be her. Sure, today she looked the country girl. Sure, she even tasted like a country girl—a very sexy country girl. But she wasn't. And even if she was, she was almost engaged and headed back to the city soon. Just as well. Why put himself in that position again? He was fine the way he was.

"Speaking of Granny," she said, dusting off her hands. "I'd better be getting back. Thanks for the tour and the pogo stick lesson."

She didn't mention the kiss or the blackberries.

Probably she wanted to forget that episode as much as he did.

"Wait. You need a bandage." He was surprised she didn't protest and just leave, but when he got back from the medicine chest, she was still standing there. He wrapped the bandage around her finger. Then he brought her hand to his lips and kissed her palm.

"Better?" he said.

She nodded mutely. Her eyes were the color of brown velvet, and so deep, he felt himself sinking further and further into their depths. He stood there for a long moment, staring down into them and holding her hand in his.

Then abruptly she turned, and he watched her walk down the path—her trim waist, her firm bottom, her straight shoulders and that hair, shining so brightly in the late afternoon sun, he had to shade his eyes.

He put the pogo stick back in the barn and closed the door without looking around at the half-finished projects. They just made him feel guilty and restless. He should never have shown her around. She was only being polite. But if he hadn't, she never would have bounced around on his pogo stick, and that was a sight he wouldn't forget—her nose wrinkled in concentration, her face flushed, her legs pumping up and down. Another thing he wouldn't forget, though he intended to do his damnedest, was the taste and touch of her lips. Then there were her eyes, so deep, he'd almost drowned in them. Despite the shaft of disappointment that he'd felt when she'd declined his invitation to the fair tomorrow, he was relieved. This whole thing was too sudden, too strange and too much to handle.

When Amelia got back to the cottage, Granny had a pot of soup simmering on the stove. She was back on the couch, though, and pooh-poohed Amelia's concern that she was doing too much.

"Sorry I took so long," Amelia said. "Your neighbor showed me around his barn."

"Really?" Granny's eyes widened. Amelia was afraid she'd read too much into this development. Sure enough, Granny beamed her approval. "And you saw what a great talent he is, and how sad it is he's not working."

"You're right. Actually, in certain circles, he's famous. I read about him on the Internet."

Granny leaned forward on the couch. "Your lips are purple."

Amelia started guiltily. "Oh, that's from the blackberries along the path."

Granny nodded, but the look in her bright eyes told Amelia she knew more than she'd been told. Then Granny changed the subject. "Did he say anything about working again?"

"Not really, except he did mention wanting to do some research."

"That's good, very good," Granny said, rubbing her blue-veined hands together. "We must do everything we can to encourage him. By the way, I had a call from the home-help people over in Grandville. They're coming here tomorrow to do some physical therapy and set up some special equipment for me, hand bars for the bathtub, things like that. I told them about you and they suggested you take the day off. That's one of their functions—to give the caregiver a day off."

"You mean you don't want me here?" Amelia knew as soon as the words were out of her mouth that she was sounding like the petulant child she once was.

"Now, Amelia—"

"That's fine," she said quickly. "I can get some work done."

"Work? On your day off?"

Amelia didn't say anything. Was this really just a coincidence that Granny was giving her the day off and Brian wanted to take her to a carnival? It had to be. Besides, what would her parents say, what would her colleagues say, if they knew she was going to a county fair instead of working? It was a silly idea. It was a perfect chance to work. Then why did she feel cheated? Why did she feel this was indeed a vacation and she deserved to have some fun? It was a childish notion.

After dinner, Granny turned on her favorite sitcom and Amelia wandered outside in the twilight. What was to be gained by going to a fair, she asked herself as she walked through Granny's vegetable garden, ostensibly looking for ripe tomatoes, but mostly just occasionally stooping to yank at an errant weed.

She could list the negatives on one hand. First, she would be spending more time than necessary with the admittedly attractive Brian Wolf, which might possibly help him in his so-called research, but would not help her in doing any productive work. Second, she would be giving her grandmother false hopes that this was an important step forward in getting the two of them together. Third, she was afraid she might make a fool of herself on the roller coaster by getting sick. Fourth, she was afraid he might kiss her again, and fifth, she might enjoy it even more than today's kiss and kiss him back. Again. She was not in the market for a summer romance. She had a boyfriend, she reminded herself. A little late for a reminder, but nonetheless… She was not cut out to be anybody's muse, either. If he wanted to get back to work, he would. Nobody could force anybody else to do something against their will. Especially not her.

All those reasons, and yet, the next thing Amelia knew she'd sneaked back into the house to get her cell phone, and called Brian. When she heard his deep voice answer, her heart started pounding, and she almost lost her nerve and hung up. What was she doing? At best, this could be a summer romance, at worst, an embarrassing, inconvenient encounter.

"I, uh… About that trip to the fair to ride the roller coaster…"

"Don't worry. It was just a suggestion. I understand perfectly."

"You do?"

"Of course. You came to take care of your grandmother. When I suggested it, I wasn't thinking."

She felt a cold shiver of disappointment. He was glad she wasn't coming. He hadn't really wanted her to go with him at all. "Are you going anyway?"

"Probably not."

"Well that's too bad."

He paused.

"Because," she continued, "Granny will be taken care of tomorrow and I could go with, if, that is, you were still going. But if you're not…" What was wrong with her? She was babbling like an idiot.

"I'll pick you up at nine," he said tersely, and then he hung up. She stood there as night fell in the garden, listening to the crickets and the far-off sound of the laugh track from Granny's program, and she had the strangest feeling that she'd turned a corner and there was no going back. It was ridiculous. She was making too much of this. She was simply going to a county fair with a friend of Granny's. Then why was she breathing so hard? Why was her palm sticking to her phone?

She went back in the house, made a cup of frothy cappuccino for both her and Granny and watched a program with her grandmother. She would have been hard put, however, to say what the program had been about and who'd been in it.

Her mind wandered to the man she'd spent the day with. She thought about how peaceful he'd looked sleeping in the sun, and how energetic he'd been demonstrating the pogo stick. She thought about his hands, the gentle way he touched her finger, the way he traced the outline of her cheek, the way he kissed her so hungrily, as if he'd been starving for a long time. But why? He was attractive, creative, well-to-do, unattached. What had happened to make him seal himself off? And what would it take to get him to open up? Oh, yes, he'd started today. But then he'd shut down again. What would happen tomorrow? She shivered in anticipation, and Granny, always perceptive—sometimes too perceptive—handed her a hand-knit afghan from the couch without taking her eyes from the screen.

The next morning, Amelia had to tell Granny where she was going. But Granny was careful not to show any more enthusiasm than was necessary. After a brief pause, during which Granny digested the news, she just said, "Have a nice time." And then added, "Take a sweater. It gets cool at night." As if she'd be gone into the evening. How long did it take to ride a roller coaster?

Either Granny had changed her mind about matchmaking, or she'd decided to cool it. Whatever it was, Amelia was grateful.

"You look very nice," Granny said, her head tilted to one side.

Uh-oh. If Granny thought she looked nice, maybe she ought to change. Amelia looked down at her bright, hip-hugging, patterned capri pants and lavender knit shirt. What did it matter how she looked? It was not her intent to impress or seduce Brian Wolf. She was simply accompanying him on a research trip.

"Don't hurry back," Granny insisted. "The home-help workers are bringing two square meals." Just then, Brian drove up in his truck, and Granny waved to him through the window. "There he is, that handsome devil. Don't keep him waiting. And remember—"

"I know, act helpless."

"That's not what I was going to say," Granny said, pursing her lips. "Just relax. Have a good time."

Amelia kissed her on the cheek, then hurried out the door before Granny could give her any more advice. With her stomach doing flip-flops, she felt as if she were on a first date or going to a prom. Brian reinforced the feeling by opening the truck door for her and giving her a long, appreciative look.

Maybe she'd worn the right things after all. No matter how much she protested, maybe this was their first date. She bit her lip and gave herself a strong warning. Get real. First *and* last, she told herself.

Then he spoiled the effect by saying, "What, no cell phone?"

"It's Sunday," she said. "I'm taking the day off."

"Trying to recapture your lost childhood."

She couldn't have put it better herself. That way, it had nothing to do with him.

"If it's not too late." But it was too late. She was crazy if she thought she could be a child again. She didn't want to. She was a grown-up with responsibilities, duties and all the perks of adulthood. She was also on vacation, she reminded herself. And on vacation, anything could happen.

Chapter Six

"What made you change your mind?" Brian asked after he pulled out onto the highway.

She slanted a look in his direction. He was wearing khaki pants and a blue chambray work shirt which made his eyes look bluer than ever. He could be anybody—a day laborer; a farmer or a physically fit, famous inventor of children's toys who, for some reason, had dropped out of society. "I thought I told you. Granny's home-help workers are coming today and I wasn't needed. What made you change yours?"

"What do you mean?"

"You said 'probably not,' when I asked if you were still going, and you didn't sound happy about my coming along."

"You're wrong. I am happy. I just have a different way of showing it."

She shrugged. That was the understatement of the year. "If this is happy, I'd hate to see you when you're sad."

He shot her a reluctant smile that broadened when she smiled back. Then she leaned back in the bucket seat of his truck and rolled down the window to catch the fresh breeze and the scent of pine trees.

"You'll be glad to know Granny has backed off," Amelia said. "She didn't say a word to me when I told her where I was going."

"How did that happen? Did you tell her you were waiting for Prince Charming, and no one else would do?"

"She thinks you *are* Prince Charming."

"That's what happens when you bury yourself in the country away from civilization," he said. "You lose your perspective."

"Is that what happened to you?" she asked lightly.

"I don't want to talk about what happened to me." His voice had an edge to it. When would she learn? When would she just accept the fact that she was never going to know his story?

"Sorry." She wasn't sorry she'd asked—how would anyone find out anything if they didn't ask?— but she was sorry she'd broken the mood. Now she'd put him on the defensive again. She put her hand on his arm. "Look, Brian, I really don't care what happened to you in the past. I know you're a brilliant inventor, a good neighbor and that you must have a good reason for having stopped working. I have a feeling you'll start up again someday."

"What makes you think that?" he asked.

"Because of all that stuff in your barn. Because you're too young and too talented to just pick berries and watch sunsets. And because you're here, on your way to do research at a county fair."

"What if I made that up just to spend the day with you?"

She blinked and dropped her hand from his arm. She felt a flush creep up her face. "You're not serious!"

"Gotcha," he said.

She laughed, and the tension between them dissolved. "Whatever your reasons, we're on our way, and you might have to go on the roller coaster by yourself, because frankly, I'm scared to death at the very thought." She was even more scared as they approached the fairgrounds and entered the parking lot.

He parked his truck, and they got out and headed for the entrance gates, along with throngs of other people. Screams and laughter came floating across the fairgrounds.

"I'll hold your hand," he said, reaching for her hand.

"I don't think that will work," she said, "if I'm on the ground and you're in the air." She was still scared of the ride ahead, but with her hand in his, she felt young and free and a little giddy. Her first fair, her first summer vacation in years and her first fling, if that was what you called this strange relationship with this strange man. Not that she believed that flirtatious remark he'd made. But still, she felt as if she were a teenager, and anything was possible. Anything at all.

She walked past pens of livestock with the names of local farmers inscribed, their animals wearing blue ribbons. They walked past ringtoss games and shooting galleries, and finally they came to the Ferris Wheel. Amelia craned her neck to watch the people sitting on their seats high above them on the huge metal structure. If she weren't afraid of heights, she'd be willing to try that instead of the roller coaster. But they passed it by and kept walking until they came to the giant monster, twice as big as she'd imagined, twice as high and twice as scary. Loud screams from above filled the air as the roller coaster dipped and climbed over the crowd. When it stopped, dazed young people staggered off, laughing, gasping for breath, clinging to each other, their hair standing on end.

"Oh, no," Amelia said, her heart in her throat. "I don't think—"

"Don't think," he said, and went to buy the tickets. "This is not the time to think. Just feel."

She did feel. She felt scared, nervous, worried

and downright terrified. Feelings she didn't want to share with him. She wanted him to think she was brave and fearless. Hah.

As they stood in line, waiting for the giant torture machine to stop and let them enter one of the cars, Amelia was positive she could not get on. She tried to think of excuses—she could faint, throw up or just run away. Brian's eyes were fixed intently on the roller coaster, and she had the feeling he'd forgotten she was even there. Maybe he wouldn't mind going alone. "Aren't you the least bit scared?" she asked, wrapping her arms around her waist.

"Of what?" he asked. "I checked on the safety stats. They have a very good record."

"No fatalities? That's reassuring," she said drily. "I'm not afraid of dying, I'm afraid of…"

"Yes?" He tore his eyes away from the behemoth above them and looked down into her eyes so intently, she forgot what she'd been about to say. Hot shivers raced up her spine, and all he'd done was look at her with those incredible blue eyes of his. Coming on this trip today had not been a good idea. He knew it. That's why he'd tried to ditch the plan. But she'd insisted. Why? What was wrong with her? Couldn't she smell trouble when it was right under her nose? It must be the atmosphere, the altitude, the change of scene, because this wasn't like her at all. Taking the day off, just because it was Sunday? Cavorting with a strange man? No, this couldn't be Amelia.

The look in his eyes told her he hadn't forgotten about her after all. Whatever it was she was afraid of, she was more afraid of the effect he had on her than a thousand roller coasters. The important thing was not to let it show. Act normal. Or as normal as possible with a roller coaster overhead.

"I guess I'm just afraid of being afraid."

"That's reasonable," he said, taking her hand again. What if he pulled her into the car with him? Now how was she going to get out of this? "Everyone's afraid of the unknown. But it's fun, it's exciting and a thrill. You'll just have to trust me."

She nodded, unable to speak. What was there to say? *I don't* trust *you. You don't know what a wimp I am, and I'd rather not have you, or anyone, know. That's why I'm staying on the ground.*

"If God had wanted us to fly around in the air, wouldn't he have given us wings?" she asked, her eyes on the line ahead of them, which was shrinking until there were only a handful of people between them and the terror that lay ahead of them.

"He gave us the smarts to make machines to take us up in the air, to conquer gravity."

"Not me. I don't want to conquer gravity."

"Really? You really don't want to go?"

The look in his eyes was one of disappointment.

She'd led him on. She'd asked to come. She'd given him the impression that she was up for adventure. She'd ridden a pogo stick and now…

"Well, I just…"

Then it was there. The moment of truth. The little car stopped. The door opened. The people ahead of them jumped in. Brian shot her a quick, questioning look. She had an instant to say no, but she didn't. Instead she hopped into the front seat with him and sat back while he fastened the seat belts around them.

"What luck," he said, his eyes gleaming. "I can't believe we got the front seats. They're the best." He covered her hand with his. "Relax."

For a few minutes, she actually did relax as they rose slowly, slowly up in the air. Maybe this wouldn't be so bad after all.

Click, click, click.

"Hear that? That's the sound of a cog. We're being pulled up by a gear," he explained, twisting his head around for a better look at the machinery.

Very gingerly, Amelia looked over the edge and watched the crowd get smaller and smaller as they climbed slowly upward, each little person turning into a tiny ant way below them. It wasn't so bad, she thought. Not so far.

Now they were at the top and, suddenly, there was nothing between them and the ground below. The tracks fell away and were gone. They were looking straight down. Amelia gasped. They plunged. The air was full of screams, hers and others'. Screams behind her, screams all around her. Her stomach rose to her throat. Seconds later, they hit bottom. Her stomach felt like lead. The blood had left her head, and she felt as if her body were floating above her.

"You okay?" he asked.

"Fine," she lied. "Just fine."

"Because that was nothing."

She looked around. There were cars going over loops, people hanging upside down and screaming. There was a spiral corkscrew in her future. She saw he was right—that last part had been nothing—and she wanted to get off. She had to get off. But she couldn't. At least she didn't have to look. She buried her face in Brian's shoulder. He put his arm around her. She closed her eyes and held on for dear life.

After more loops—each one more terrifying than the last—after an eternity of pure heart-stopping thrills, they arrived back on earth. She stumbled out of the car, feeling dizzy and disoriented. Her stomach was somewhere up there in the air. Some day she hoped to have it back.

She staggered, hand in hand with Brian, toward a grassy field, to a labeled picnic area where families were spread out on blankets, eating and soaking up the sun. Some kids were throwing Frisbees. Others were listening to a baseball game on a loud radio. She lay on the grass on her back and closed her eyes.

"How did you like it?" he asked.

"Terrifying," she murmured.

"What part did you like best?" he asked.

"The part where we got off."

"Are you sorry you went?"

"Oh, no," she lied. "How about you?"

"I wasn't really able to enjoy it. I was paying too much attention to you."

"Me?"

"You should have seen the look on your face."

"All right, so I was scared. What did you expect?"

"I expected you to be scared. I also noticed the mechanics. I got a few ideas."

"I'm glad for you," she said. She tried to sit up but she couldn't. The world was spinning around, and wouldn't stop. She groaned.

"What do you want? A hot dog? Cotton candy? Something to drink?" She groaned again. "I shouldn't have made you go."

"Yes, you should." She sat up slowly and looked at him. "There's something about facing your worst fears. I did it, and I'm still alive."

"You sound surprised. You look pale. I'm going to get you something to drink."

He left her there on the grass to recover. She'd told him she'd faced her worst fears, but was riding a roller coaster really her worst fear? Wasn't it more about failure? And wasn't her second-worst fear about making a mistake? About making a commitment to one man and then regretting it for the rest of her life? Wasn't that why she worked so hard, and why she'd avoided telling Jeff she would marry him? Was it possible the roller-coaster ride had jarred some sense into her head? Or had it merely planted some long-standing questions there, questions that had no ready answers?

When Brian came back with hot dogs and lemonade, she was ready to rejoin the ranks of the living. She was actually hungry and very thirsty.

"Good girl," he said, patting her on the head.

"You sound like you're talking to your dog," she said, sipping her lemonade. "You never would have forced Dante to go on a ride like that."

"I didn't force you. You had free will to get on or not. Come on, you're proud of yourself, aren't you? I know you. You're the type who likes a challenge."

He was right. She took chances. Was that why she was here today? "How do you know?"

"It's written all over your face," he said, tracing the outline of her face with his fingers.

She swallowed hard. He had the most amazing ability to make her feel as if she were melting into a puddle in the sun. She had to change the subject, away from her, back to him. She didn't want to be analyzed. Maybe she was afraid to find out what made her tick. Maybe she was more afraid that he'd find out.

"What made you want to invent toys?" she asked.

"Instead of, say, kitchen gadgets?" he asked. "Like a dishwasher that recycles the plates back onto the shelves when they're clean, or an orange-juice squeezer that spits out the skin and turns it into spot remover?"

"You could do that?"

"No. Besides, toys are fun. Everybody likes toys. Even adults. Especially me. They take us back to a happier time when we were young and naive. One thing for sure, I had some naive ideas."

"Like?" she suggested, holding her breath. She noticed this time he hadn't mentioned making toys for his own kids. Was he really going to confide in her?

"My most naive idea was that marriage is a commitment. Then there was the one that goes real love lasts a lifetime."

"It does for some people," she said. "Granny and Grandpa had a wonderful life together."

"What was their secret?"

"I wish I knew," she said, shaking her head.

"Want my advice? Don't marry that guy until you find out."

"Thanks for the advice. But you don't even know him." The nerve of the man. Whether she married Jeff or not was none of his business. "Anyway, you don't seem naive to me. You seem very mature."

"Do I? That's because you don't know me."

She tilted her head and studied his face. He seemed lost in thought, and she was sorry she'd opened her mouth. She felt she was getting close to what was bothering him, and now he'd shut down again.

"No, I don't," she murmured. She didn't know him at all. But she wanted to. She wanted to badly. She wanted to know what had made him stop working, and she didn't want to hear it from someone else, like Granny. She wanted him to trust her enough to tell her himself. She thought it would unlock the secret to his past. "What I do know is that you're here today for a reason. You came to do research for your toy roller coaster. At least, that's what you said."

"That was the plan," he said. "But instead I've learned more than I bargained for." Brian had learned something about the mechanics of the roller coaster, but even more, he'd learned that he liked having Amelia's face buried against his shoulder. He'd been on roller coasters by himself—because Natalie wouldn't go—and this was better. He liked putting his arm around Amelia and feeling her body melt into his. He liked watching her face her fears and overcome them. But could he do the same? More to the point, should he? What the hell. He was with an incredible woman today. She was gutsy and determined, and she was just beginning to discover her inner child. She'd be going back to her real life before long, and that inner child might be buried again for good. He might or might not go back to his real life. Nevertheless, it was a beautiful day, and it was a shame to waste it. All around them, people were having fun. Why shouldn't they? "Now that we're here, let's forget about work. Don't look so shocked. You're taking the day off, remember?"

She nodded, got to her feet and dusted off her pants. She reached down to pick up the paper wrappers as a boy on a bicycle zoomed by, doing a wheelie.

Brian watched the kid crisscross the grass, wondering if the boy would like his pogo stick or his toy roller coaster. Wondering if he'd ever have his own kids who'd try out his toys and give him instant feedback. Not at the rate he was going. But it no longer mattered. That was a dream that had died a long time ago.

Amelia watched Brian watch the boy on the bike. "I suppose you have plans for a new and improved bike, too?" she asked.

"I've done some work on it," he said. But he didn't want to think about that now. He grabbed her arm. "Let's go check out the shooting gallery."

There, he won a huge stuffed panda, which Amelia carried around with her for the rest of the day. She looked as pleased as if he'd given her a diamond necklace. Probably because she'd never had toys.

Then they went to the demo derby, where real cars were smashed by men with hammers. For some reason that struck them both as funny. They laughed hysterically as the cars disintegrated. When their laughter subsided into awkward silence, and they wandered to the next attraction, Brian wondered if he'd lost his mind. He hadn't laughed for months, so what had gotten into him? Why now? Why here? Why her? Amelia seemed to be lost in thought, also, as if she were wondering if she'd slipped a cog up there on the roller coaster.

"It wasn't that funny," she remarked soberly. "It must be the aftereffects of the roller coaster. I still feel a little light-headed."

"That's it," he said, relieved, as they strolled through the home-arts tent, with tables full of jams and jellies and relishes. The sun shone on the glass jars of preserved fruits, turning them into purple, red and orange jewels.

"I'll bet you could have won something with your apple pie," he said, holding up a jar of pickles to the light.

"Think so?" she asked. "Maybe next year I'll enter."

"You're coming back next year?"

"One thing I know, I'm not going to wait until Granny gets sick to come. I really need to see her more often. I realize how much I've missed her, missed the country. Not that I could ever live here."

"Of course not," he agreed quickly. She didn't need to tell him. "No sushi bars, no nightlife, no health clubs."

"That's not what I'd miss," she said stiffly. "How shallow do you think I am?"

"Hey." He lifted his hands as if to surrender. "I'm sorry if I misjudged you. So what would you miss?"

"Work, friends, the pace of life. I'd go crazy here in the country."

"It's not for everyone," he admitted. That, he'd had to learn the hard way. "How do you feel about barbecues, city girl? Think you can handle a rack of ribs, a mess of beans and some coleslaw?"

"Of course. I'm fine now."

They found the tent where men in white shirts and red suspenders were turning huge chunks of meat on a spit. Shadows were falling over the fairgrounds, and some people were heading for the exit. They stood at the edge of the tent.

He saw Amelia sniff the air and he wondered if she was really hungry. She'd been thoroughly shaken up on that roller coaster. Then she'd eaten a hot dog. Maybe he shouldn't have insisted on her going, but if he hadn't, she'd be sorry now. She hesitated, then said, "I'm wondering if I ought to leave Granny any longer."

"I'll give her a call," he said, taking his cell phone out of his pocket.

"Wait a minute. I thought this was a day off. I didn't even know you had a cell phone."

"I do. I'm not a complete hermit, you know." He punched in the number. "Helen? It's Brian. We're still at the fair. Here's Amelia." He handed her his phone.

"Granny, how are you doing? Really? Well, that's wonderful. Yes, we're having a good time. I rode a roller coaster… I was terrified. It's getting late, so… You are…? You do? Well, all right. We'll be back in an hour or two… No, I won't… Yes, I will. 'Bye." She handed the phone back to him. "Big surprise. She doesn't want us to hurry back. She wants us to have a good time."

"You could have told her you weren't—"

"Yes, but she wouldn't have believed me. Spending the day with Prince Charming? How could I not have a good time?" She grinned at him. "Anyway, the home-help workers were there, and now a friend has dropped by with some dessert. They're gossiping and I'm not to hurry back. Of course, she'd say that if she had fallen on the other hip and was lying on the floor in pain. I'm surprised she even asked me to come and help out. Or at least, I was until I discovered her true motive. But that's Granny for you." She turned to catch a whiff of the savory meat searing on the grill that wafted their way. "I never thought I'd be hungry again, but I am."

She found a table while he picked up two plates

of barbecued ribs, potato salad, baked beans and corn bread.

They ate. They talked a little. They joked a little. Then they got serious over coffee at the next booth.

"You said you'd miss work, but you didn't say exactly what you do," he said, adding two packets of sugar to his coffee.

"I think I told you we sell software."

"You write it?"

"No, but I hire the people who do. Then I sell it to businesses."

"Are you good at it?"

She shrugged and stirred her coffee. "Just ask Granny. Hasn't she told you how brilliant I am? How I'm going to be president and CEO any day now?"

"So it's true."

"If I do everything right, maybe."

"Is that what you want?"

"I've always wanted to be a success. You see my parents… Never mind, you don't want to hear all this."

"Sure I do. It's come to my attention that I've been spending too much time alone. That I'm reduced to talking to my dog. I'm taking this opportunity to learn to communicate with my peers. If you don't mind my referring to you as my 'peer.'"

"I'm flattered," she said. "Though I'm not as good a listener as Dante, why don't you tell me about yourself?"

"There's not much to tell, really." Liar. There was too much to tell. Too much that he wanted to forget.

"Oh, come on. This is your opportunity to communicate with one of your peers."

"Okay." She sure was persistent. He'd say that for her. "I had a happy childhood, one father, one mother, one brother. I had lots of toys, but I always was tinkering with them. Taking them apart and rebuilding them. I majored in mechanical design at college, got a job with a big toy company, and quit a few years later. Went into business for myself and that's it."

"That's it?" She sounded disappointed and disbelieving. "Sounds like you left out something."

"Oh, yeah. I also got a dog and moved to the country."

"Okay," she said stiffly. She picked up her paper cup and tossed it in the trash. Then they headed for the exit and home without saying much more. So she was disappointed. Too bad. He'd told her everything he was going to tell her.

In the car, they talked about the town of Pine Mountain, of the changes there over the years, about Granny and her little cottage. They talked about everything except anything important about themselves and their former lives. Maybe he should have told her about his recent past then, as darkness fell around them, but he couldn't bring himself to do it. He wasn't ready. He might never be ready.

He wouldn't mind hearing about her life. As far as he knew, she had no dark secrets the way he did, but she didn't seem inclined to confide in him, either. He didn't blame her. So they made small talk. Maybe she was mad because he wouldn't bare his soul. He wondered how much Helen had told her. He thought he could count on his neighbor to keep his secrets. When he pulled up in front of the cottage, he noticed there was a light on in the living room.

"She's waiting up for you."

"The curtain is moving. She's looking out," Amelia said.

"Let's give her something to look at. Make her day," he said. And he pulled Amelia toward him and kissed her. Her lips were stiff, her body was tense. It was a mean trick, using Helen as an excuse, but he thought it was worth a try. He'd wanted to kiss her again since the first time in the berry patch, to see if the thrill had been because she was a novelty or because it had been so long since he'd kissed a woman. He also had an insane desire to see how she'd taste without berries on her lips.

Amelia put her hands on Brian's shoulders with the express purpose of pushing him away. *Give her something to look at!* Really, the guy was unbelievable. Did he think she was some kind of pushover? But something happened on her way to shove him away. His kiss got to her. He rang bells in her head, made her feel as if she was helplessly sliding down out of control. And before she knew it, she was kissing him back. The steering wheel was poking her ribs, but she was oblivious to the pain. She locked her hands around his neck and kissed him until she was breathless. His hands were everywhere, one cradling her head, the other wrapped around her waist. Everywhere he touched her she burned. She was scared. More scared than she'd been on the roller coaster. At the carnival, she'd known the ride would be over and she would be able to get off, but this was the kind of ride that could go on and on. If she let it. It was a wild ride that had her heart in her throat, her stomach in knots and her heart pounding. She finally came to her senses and broke the kiss.

"I think we've given Granny enough of a show for one night. That was what this was all about, wasn't it?" she asked breathlessly.

"Of course," he said, but his voice was as rough as Granny's gravel driveway.

"I think we should get our story straight," she said, smoothing her shirt, feeling a wave of regret wash over her. What was she thinking, kissing the mystery man from the country as if there were no tomorrow? In fact, tomorrow would soon come, and she'd be headed back to the city.

"What story do you mean?" he asked. It was too dark to know for sure, but she would have bet he was smiling. So this was all a joke to him, was it? While she had to go inside and face her grandmother.

"About what happened today."

"What did happen?" he asked.

She sighed. "Nothing, but she's not going to believe that."

"All right, tell her what we did."

"Up to a point," she said,

"But…" He looked at the window of the house, where a curtain fluttered and a shadow moved. "Think fast. She's seen us."

Amelia leaned against the door and opened it. Think fast? She couldn't think at all. "Good night," she said, and walked up the path. Her legs wobbled and her heart pounded against her will. It wasn't going to be easy to pretend she hadn't been kissed senseless a few minutes previously. Convincing Granny she wasn't interested in Brian would be hard, but the real challenge would be convincing herself.

Chapter Seven

"How was it?" Granny asked brightly.

Amelia tossed her sweater on a chair. "Scary. I'm never going again."

Granny's face fell.

Amelia couldn't bear to see her disappointment. She grinned. "Just kidding. The roller coaster was scary, but otherwise the fair was fun. How was your day?" Amelia asked quickly before Granny could ask for details.

"Oh, fine. The home-help workers brought me some exercise bars, gave me a shower and showed me how to use this walker here. Then my friend Jenny came by. I told her all about you. She brought some brownies. Try one."

"No thanks, Granny. We just had dinner."

"You did? You and Brian had dinner together?" Granny beamed at her as if she'd just announced their engagement.

"Just some ribs at the barbecue tent at the fair," Amelia said.

"Oh." Granny was studying Amelia so intently from behind her glasses that Amelia was afraid her hair was standing on end or her shirt was hanging out of her pants or her face was scraped raw by razor burn or just that she looked as guilty as she felt.

She was grateful for the shaded lamps in the living room. Still, Granny's eyes were sharp and her intuition hadn't faded one bit. She'd always known what Amelia had been up to as a child, whether she'd been trying to sneak another cookie or borrowing Granny's perfume. No, there was no fooling her. Still, Amelia had to try. It was for Granny's own good. If she really thought she could force her neighbor to fall for her granddaughter, she needed to face reality or risk severe disappointment.

"What can I do for you before I turn in?" Amelia asked.

"Nothing, dear. You go to bed. I'm just glad you recovered from that roller-coaster ride. Brian should never have taken you on it. What was wrong with the other rides—a Ferris Wheel, for instance?"

"Or a merry-go-round? Granny, I'm a big girl. I had to give it a try."

"Of course you did. And I'm proud of you."

"I see you have a doctor's appointment tomorrow, right?" Amelia asked, picking up Granny's calendar.

"Yes, but I'm afraid I can't get my hip into your car, so Brian is going to take me in his truck. It's all about the angle."

"But, Granny, I thought I was…" Useful. Amelia thought she'd be useful, but she was beginning to feel that she wasn't needed at all. Why hadn't Brian said anything about taking Granny in his truck? Because she'd just invented it?

"Of course, you'll come along," Granny said. "I want you to meet my doctor."

"Why, is he single?" Amelia asked drily.

Granny chuckled. "Honestly, dear, you're making me out to be some kind of matchmaker. He's happily married and he has five grandchildren."

"Then I'd love to meet him. I want to hear what he has to say about you."

"Run along and get your beauty rest, then," Granny said. "Not that you need it."

Amelia nodded.

Upstairs, with the windows wide open thanks to Brian and his tool kit, the night air blew through the little bedroom. Amelia got ready for bed and gazed across the trees to the house where he lived. The same light she'd seen last night was on, and she could almost see him at his desk, writing notes on his computer about the roller coaster. Then his light went out. And back on. He was signaling her. She flipped her light out and on again. A strange warmth filled her heart. If he wanted to communicate with her, he could have picked up the phone and called her, but he didn't. Signaling was something she might have done as a child, if she'd known someone who lived there, but she hadn't. There was something so simple, so direct about the process, she smiled into the darkness.

She watched and waited, but his light came on and stayed on. Amelia thought she'd be so tired, she'd fall asleep right away. Instead, she felt awake and alert. Instead of staring off in the distance, trying to catch a glimpse of him, which was not productive, she opened her briefcase. If she couldn't sleep, why not get some work done? She'd call the office tomorrow and see what was happening.

But the papers in her briefcase didn't hold her interest. In fact, they could have been written in a foreign language, for all they meant to her. She kept thinking of the fair, the crowds of happy people, the music, the smells—of farm animals and hay, of roasting meat—the feel of Brian's arm around her as they went free-falling through space. The taste of his lips on hers. The feel of his arms around her.

She put the papers away, closed her briefcase and turned off her light. His was still on. She pulled the blanket over her head and tried to pretend she didn't know he was close by in his house through the woods. Tried to pretend she didn't feel her whole body tingling with awareness. Tried to forget she'd spent a truly memorable day with him, during which she'd run the gamut of emotions—from fear to pleasure to passion.

When Amelia awoke the next day, she headed straight to her phone—refusing to look out the window—and placed a call to the office. No one was there. So much for her staff filling in for her. It was nearly nine o'clock. Where were they? After she helped Granny get dressed for her appointment and made her a piece of toast, she finally got hold of her assistant and learned that there was panic in the office. The CEO was on vacation, and all the computers were down. With one eye on the kitchen clock, Amelia tried to call the client who was going ballistic over technical failure. No one at Frantz and Fotre was taking any calls. It made her nervous. The company couldn't afford to lose a single client. Not in this business climate. It was almost time to leave, and she hadn't accomplished anything. She should be taking care of the computer problem. Of course, she could let Brian take Granny to the doctor. No, that wouldn't do.

Still wearing her bathrobe, she bolted up the stairs at the sound of Brian's truck outside. She grabbed a

pair of white linen capri pants and a black knit shirt
from her still-packed suitcase, got dressed and hurried back downstairs. Why she should feel embarrassed at seeing Brian this morning, she didn't know.
It was just a kiss, that was all. Or was it? Her heart
was pounding, and it wasn't from running up and
down the stairs. He, on the other hand, looked more
cheerful than she'd ever seen him. And completely
calm and composed. Granny remarked on it.

"Why, Brian," Granny said, "you look very handsome today. Doesn't he, Amelia?"

Amelia almost laughed. Her grandmother was
unstoppable. "He certainly does," she admitted.
"There's nothing like a day at the fair to bring out the
best in a person."

Brian raised one eyebrow. She didn't know what
that meant, but at least he didn't frown at her.

Amelia was squeezed into the back seat of Brian's
truck while Granny and her new hip were tilted at the
appropriate angle in the passenger seat. Granny was
in good spirits, remarking on the neighbors' vegetable gardens and pointing out their horses behind the
wooden fences to Amelia, as enthusiastic as if she
were a real estate agent trying to sell some property.
One would have thought she'd been housebound for
months instead of days.

At the doctor's office in the nearby town of Wil-
ford—named for a one-time gold prospector and

filled with tourist shops selling geodes and other native rocks dug from the nearby hills, as well as hand-stitched moccasins—Amelia went into the examining room while Brian stayed in the waiting room. The doctor was pleased with Granny's progress and told her she could walk on level surfaces, but not stairs.

"You're fortunate to have your granddaughter with you," Dr. Campbell said.

"I know," Granny said. "I told her I didn't need someone, but she insisted on coming. That's the way she is."

Amelia smiled modestly.

"How long will you be here?" the doctor asked her.

"As long as she needs me," Amelia said.

"I think with the home-help people coming three times a week, your grandmother could probably cope on her own at this point."

"What?" Granny said, sitting up so quickly on the examining table, she almost lost her glasses.

Amelia took Granny's hands in hers to steady her. "Don't worry, I'm not going to rush off," she said. But she couldn't help thinking about the mess her office was in. Clients threatening to leave, computers down, staff in disarray. If she left tomorrow morning, she could be back in the city by late afternoon. It was a tempting thought.

Granny looked pale when they left the office. Worse than when they'd arrived. Worse than when

Amelia had first come to her cottage. When Brian suggested stopping at a drive-in restaurant, Granny smiled wanly.

She managed to nibble a hamburger and drink a little of her milkshake, but she didn't talk much. Brian sent Amelia a puzzled look, and she shrugged.

"What's wrong, Granny?" she asked, after they'd returned home and helped her into the house. Brian had left after stacking firewood on the front porch. He hadn't made any excuses. He hadn't needed to. After all, he wasn't obliged to hang around and account for his whereabouts. It was just that Amelia was wondering, just wondering, if the events of last night, of yesterday, had meant anything to him. He hadn't said anything, but neither had she. How could she with Granny around all the time?

"Nothing, dear, I'm fine," Granny said. "It's just...nothing. Ohh." She put one hand on her hip.

"What's wrong? It's your hip, isn't it?" Amelia asked with a worried frown. "Why didn't you tell the doctor it was bothering you?"

"It wasn't. Not then. But don't worry about me. You have enough on your mind. I couldn't help overhearing you talking on the phone this morning. You have problems of your own."

"Nothing that won't keep," Amelia said, crossing her fingers behind her back and hoping she wouldn't be struck by lightning for lying. She had problems galore, and they couldn't wait. But Granny came first. "Did you twist your hip getting out of the truck?"

"Oh, no. At least, I don't think so."

"Shall I call the doctor?" Amelia asked.

"Don't be silly. You heard what he said. I'm fine."

"But you're not. You're in pain."

"I wish Brian hadn't dashed off like that. I would have asked him...never mind."

"What? What is it?"

"Well, he has the most wonderful tea he served me one day when I stopped in to see him. It's so soothing, so calming. It's called, oh, I can't remember— something Chinese. It's made from herbs. The Chinese use it for medicinal purposes."

"I'll call him. Maybe he could bring it over," Amelia suggested.

Granny smiled. Amelia noted that Granny looked better already. There was a little color in her cheeks and her eyes looked brighter. But was it the thought of the tea or the thought of Brian coming by? Of course he agreed to bring the tea. Whatever the cause, the effect on Granny was a positive one. And when Brian walked in the door, Granny really perked up.

Amelia looked at her with surprise. Was she faking this latest setback? Of course not. Why would she do that? Why, indeed? For the same reason she was manufacturing all these reasons for Amelia to go to Brian's house. She was determined to get them together.

Amelia stood and watched while Brian brewed a pot of his special tea. She had to admit he knew his way around a kitchen, especially Granny's. In a few minutes, he had a pot of fragrant, steaming tea on the table. He poured three cups and, without even asking, spooned honey into each of them.

"Thank you, Brian," Granny said sweetly from the couch. "I feel better already. Now you two run along outside. It's time for my soap opera."

"I didn't know you watched the soaps," Amelia said. In fact, she knew for certain that Granny hated the soaps. She made fun of "people who had nothing better to do than watch that drivel."

"Normally I don't, but since I've been laid up, I've gotten hooked on one called *The Beverly Hills Heroes*. Don't look down your nose, Amelia, it's better than those reality shows you young people watch these days."

"I don't watch reality shows, Granny," Amelia said indignantly.

"Of course not. Your parents would never approve." Granny picked up the remote control and waved the two of them away.

Amelia looked at Brian. He gave her a half smile. He knew perfectly well what Granny was up to, and so did she. So they walked out the front door onto the patio and sat down in Granny's lounge chairs. Sure enough, the television was on in the background. Maybe she really did watch the soaps. At least, she was watching them today.

Amelia sipped her tea. She didn't know what else to do. Since he'd made it, she could hardly dump it on the ground. It was too hot out for hot tea but that would be rude.

"So your parents don't approve of lightweight TV any more than they do of toys," Brian said.

"That doesn't mean I can't watch it," Amelia said. "Or that I can't use a pogo stick or ride a roller coaster. They don't control my life anymore."

"Don't they?" he asked.

"Of course not. I'm my own person. I lead my own life. I don't even see them that much."

"They must be proud of you, succeeding in such a competitive field."

"It's what they expected. Actually, they expected me to be a CEO by now."

"Why aren't you?" he asked.

"That's what they want to know. Am I not working hard enough? Not motivated? Distracted?"

"Well?"

She sighed. She had no answer for him, nor for herself. She'd been passed over for the job just last year, so she'd moved to another company. Would it happen soon? Was it ever going to happen?

"Could it be it's not what you want, but what they want for you?"

"Of course not. You don't know anything about me, or you wouldn't say that."

"Do they know you any better?"

"Good question. Sometimes I wonder."

"You said they were gone a lot, left you here during the summers."

"Yes, but they returned by fall to make sure I got back on track during the school year, so I could get into the right high school, then the right college and, of course, on to get my MBA."

He whistled. "I'm impressed. I have no head for business. My patent attorney and my accountant have to handle everything. I'd be better off if I took more of an interest in the business side of my career."

"Why should you? You're creative. Right brain. Not many people are both."

"I take it you were an only child."

"I was a *lonely* only child. I hated it. If I ever get married and have any red-haired kids, I'm going to have more than one."

"How does your boyfriend feel about that?" he asked tightly.

"Jeff?" She was startled by his question. "I don't know. I've never asked him." Why hadn't she? Was it because she really couldn't see herself marrying him? This man that she'd only met a few days ago was making her question everything in her life—her job, and now her almost fiancé. It was disturbing. She didn't need any more uncertainty in her life. She quickly changed the subject. "What about you? Didn't you tell me you were making those toys with your own kids in mind?"

There was a long silence while Amelia thought she'd probed too much, asked too many questions. Maybe he was offended, or maybe just reluctant to confide in a stranger. Considering the warning signs on his gate and his whole attitude the first time she'd met him, that would be no surprise She was ready to apologize when he finally spoke.

"Did I say that? Wishful thinking, I guess. But when my wife left, over a year ago, and suddenly there were no kids in my future, I quit working. I didn't see the point. Ridiculous, really, to make it so personal. It was a business."

Wife? She held her breath and pretended that he hadn't just made a huge breakthrough. He'd confided in her. He'd mentioned kids before, but no wife. Now she knew that the woman had left him. No wonder he was hurt. No wonder he'd buried himself. She responded to his last remark.

"Sure, it was a business, but a creative one that requires a certain frame of mind. I know, I deal with programmers, and when they're upset about something in their lives, they can't work. It's my job to focus their energy and spark their creativity."

"I'll bet you're good at it," he said with such frank admiration in his eyes it made her blush.

"I try," she said.

"Creative or not, the reality is, I was making toys to sell to the masses, so it shouldn't have made a difference if I didn't have any kids in my life. But somehow, I just couldn't keep doing it." He shrugged as if it didn't matter, but the troubled look in his deepset eyes and the lines in his forehead told her that the trauma, whatever it was, was still bothering him.

"You said this was over a year ago?" she asked carefully.

He looked at his watch. "Fourteen months. But who's counting?"

"I'm sorry," she said.

"Don't be. I'm not. Not anymore."

Amelia edged her chair closer to his. She wanted to reach out and put her hand on his arm. She wanted to tell him how well he was doing. But she was afraid he didn't want her sympathy. She was afraid he'd jump up and make some excuse to disappear down that path to his house, and she'd never see him again. Anytime now, he could revert to his hostile, hermit-like self. So she sat there, afraid to move or say anything, until he got to his feet. She held her breath. He walked toward Granny's lavender bushes that lined her path, broke off a stem and stuck it in his pocket. Then he walked back across the patio, a faraway look in his eyes.

"Since you've arrived, I've hardly thought about her. I'd lost interest in my work, as you noticed, but now I can't wait to get back to my barn and think about what to do next." He shook his head. "I don't know why, or what you've done, but I feel like a different person."

"Nothing," she said softly. "If anyone's done anything, it's you. You were ready, you just didn't know it."

"I don't think so. Or if I was ready, I couldn't act on it. Somebody had to show me. Somebody had to believe in me."

Amelia held her breath.

"You," he said, holding her by the shoulders and looking deep into her eyes. A shiver ran up Amelia's spine. Her eyes locked with his, and for a long moment, she was conscious of nothing but him and the faint buzz of the bees in the background.

"She didn't just leave," he said suddenly.

Amelia blinked. He dropped his hands from her shoulders. She just looked at him, waiting, hoping he'd continue.

Brian didn't want to talk about his ex-wife. It was too painful. A few people knew—Helen for one, and his attorney for another, because he'd handled the formalities. So why was he on the verge of confiding in an almost-total stranger? Was it the look in her eyes, unwavering and nonjudgmental? Or was it the fact that she'd confided in him? That he knew so much about her, but she knew nothing about him?

Helen could have told her, but he knew she hadn't. He trusted Helen with his secrets more than anyone. It gave him a warm feeling to realize that even knowing everything about him, Helen was still apparently willing to throw him and her precious granddaughter together. Not that that was ever going to work, but still…

Or was the real reason that he'd kissed her last night and she'd kissed him back? She'd kissed him with so much fervor, without even knowing anything about him, or not much, anyway. Not the important stuff. Or was it because he couldn't stop thinking about her? Was it because he wanted to kiss her again, right now, in the garden, with the smell of lavender under his nose and the bittersweet taste of Chinese herbal tea lingering on his tongue?

He wanted to grab her and crush her body to his. To wrap his arms around her and feel her breasts pressed against his chest. To bury his face in her beautiful, shiny hair and smell the fragrance of her soft skin. He wanted to lose himself for a few minutes, or a few hours, and forget the past. Was that so wrong?

The psychiatrist he'd gone to after Natalie had left would say no, of course not. In fact, he'd be pleased to hear it. To a professional analyst, it might sound like the first steps on the road to recovery. Or maybe the first step was the day Amelia had appeared at his door. Maybe it was just that his dormant lust had returned, and when Amelia left, it would leave, too. But what the hell? This was a fling. For her. For him. A rare departure for both of them. She was a workaholic with an almost fiancé. And he? He didn't know how to trust anymore. Maybe that's why he had to tell somebody about himself. Not *somebody*. Her.

"She hated it here," he blurted. "I knew that. I don't know why I expected any different. It was just…" He spread his hands in a gesture of futility. "A ridiculous idea, bringing somebody like her to live here. She was out of her element—no friends, no fun, no work. Just me, and I was certainly no fun. I was working night and day on a new toy. Under deadline from the manufacturer. Looking back, I don't know what I was thinking to imagine it would work." He paced back and forth across the porch.

"But she had to think that, too, or she wouldn't have come," Amelia said, wrapping her arms around her waist.

He stopped pacing to look her in the eye. "I talked her into it. I told her it was beautiful up here."

"It is."

"I told her it was a great place to raise a family. Toys, kids, the creek, the outdoors."

"It is," Amelia said. "It really is."

Brian continued as if she hadn't spoken. Now that he'd begun, he had to finish the story. He had to tell Amelia everything. "When I saw this place a few years ago, all I could think about was bringing a wife here, having kids, making toys for them, working at home, enjoying the country. I fooled myself into thinking it would work. I wanted to make Natalie into someone she wasn't. I'll never do that again. Because it wasn't enough for her. She needed more than I could give her. I thought she'd make friends, find some kind of work, some kind of happiness."

"I gather she didn't find any of those things."

"She found a friend," he said stiffly.

Amelia didn't say anything, she just looked at him.

"He worked at a health club in Rosewood, over the hill. She went there to work out. It was the only thing she looked forward to. He was her personal trainer." Brian paused and raked one hand through his hair. He studied Amelia for a long moment. There was no going back now. He had to tell the whole story. He hoped she wouldn't pity him. He didn't want or need pity. "One night, she left with him. Left for good. Didn't tell me to my face, just left me a note. It was a foggy night. They were speeding, and crashed into a redwood tree halfway down the hill. They were both killed instantly."

"Oh, my God. Brian, I'm so sorry." Her eyes filled with tears. But it wasn't pity he saw in her eyes, it was sympathy. There was a difference. It was more than sympathy, it was understanding and caring. She put her arms around his waist and hugged him. He felt a hard knot in his chest dissolve as he held her tight and buried his face in her hair. He didn't know if it was because he'd finally told someone, or if it was just that time really did heal all wounds or…or was it something else? Was it her? Did it take another woman to make him lose his guilt for ignoring Natalie, his sorrow over his failed marriage? He didn't want to think about it. He just wanted to feel. And what he felt was lust, passion and the life force coming back.

He kissed her then, one hand laced through her hair, supporting her head, the other on the small of her back. She felt so good, so right in his arms, he forgot about Helen inside the house. He forgot about the past and the future. He was immersed in the softness, the sweetness and the reality of the woman in his arms. His blood was pumping through his veins. He wanted nothing more than to bury himself in her body.

Amelia felt the force of his kisses, and in the back of her mind she guessed the reason—he was coming to terms with his loss. He was using her to get over it. She didn't care. She just wanted to feel the beat of his heart against hers, the thrust of his body against hers as their tongues tangled.

His hand reached under her shirt and cupped her breast. She gasped. She'd never felt like this before, never wanted to rip a man's clothes off and make love to him under the shade of an apple tree. He stroked her nipple through the satin of her bra, and she felt her knees buckle. He braced her against him, his kisses deeper, wilder than before. She matched them kiss for kiss. Her whole body thrummed with tension. She wanted him. He wanted her. It seemed so simple. She staggered backward toward the apple tree. He didn't miss a beat. He continued his barrage of kisses until she backed into the rough bark of the tree. The smell of apples filled the air. The sun filtered through the leaves. She'd never wanted anyone the way she wanted Brian. She was breathing hard. So was he.

He pulled her down to the ground, and they sprawled on their sides in the leaves, smiling at each other. He took a leaf from her hair and tucked a stray curl behind her ear.

"You have the most beautiful hair," he said roughly.

"You think so?" she asked lightly, trying to catch her breath. "You haven't called me Red lately."

That did it. It brought back the first day she'd arrived and he hadn't been able to take his eyes off her copper-colored hair. He'd wanted her then, he just couldn't admit it. But now, that one remark sent him almost over the edge.

Chapter Eight

Brian rolled over and pressed his body on top of hers. That beautiful hair framed her face like a halo. He braced his arms on the dry ground next to her shoulders and studied her face. Then the memories came flooding back—another woman, another time, a disastrous outcome. "Amelia," he said hoarsely, his mouth against her ear. "We can't do this."

"What?" She sat up, and he jumped back and got to his feet. "Why not?" she asked, looking up at him. She had to know now. Before she got any more involved. Before she made a fool of herself. Was it because of his past? Was it something she'd done? "All women aren't like your wife, you know."

"Of course not. That's not it," he said. He stuffed

his hands in his pockets. He paced back and forth. "The point is, I haven't changed. I was a lousy husband, a lousy lover."

She licked her lips. Her whole body throbbed. She'd never been kissed like that before. She'd lost track of time and space. She wrapped her arms around her knees and stared at the ground. "I find that hard to believe." Her voice shook. She couldn't control it.

"I want to think I've changed, but I haven't. Oh, I hadn't been working until the other day, but once I start, I forget everything else, everyone else."

"Fine. Go ahead. Go ahead and work. It's important to you. Forget me, forget everyone. I'll be leaving soon, anyway."

"I know. I just thought maybe…"

"Maybe what? We'd have a brief fling, a summer romance? No thanks." Of course, that's all she'd wanted until now. Now everything was different. How had it happened?

"No, no, of course not. You deserve better than that. Someone who will love you more than anything, more than their work. Even when I was in love with Natalie, she never came first. But that's just me."

"Thank you for telling me," she said drily. She stared off into the trees without seeing the breeze brushing the pine needles off them. Okay, so he wasn't capable of loving anyone more than he loved his work. Still, he had no right to jerk her around like this. One minute hot, the next cold. One minute he couldn't keep his hands off her, the next minute he was back to the man she'd met that first day—cool, aloof, distant.

He reached for her hands and pulled her to her feet. Her knees were still weak, but she yanked her hands from his, straightened her shoulders and looked him straight in the eye. "I'm going to see about Granny."

He nodded. His mouth was twisted into a semismile, but his eyes were deep and dark, with no hint of humor. Damn it, she felt sorry for him. But he didn't need her pity, and he sure didn't want it, so why bother? Let him suffer by himself. He didn't follow her. She didn't turn around to see if he was still there. She didn't care.

When she walked into the cottage, Granny was at the kitchen sink, washing some red-leaf lettuce under cold water.

"Let me do that," Amelia said, taking it out of her hand. "You should be lying down. You said you were having pain."

"Oh, I'm feeling much better," Granny said. She sure looked better. The color was back in her cheeks and her eyes were bright. "You know, the doctor said I could get around. The exercise would be good for me. Where's Brian?"

"He's gone home."

Granny's face fell. She suddenly aged about twenty years. "But I thought you were getting along so well. I thought he'd stay for dinner."

Amelia understood in a flash that Granny had witnessed the scene out on the porch, and maybe the one under the apple tree, and of course, had jumped to the wrong conclusions. As had Amelia. It was time to set her straight.

"He told me what happened," Amelia said.

"I knew he would," Granny said, leaving the lettuce and walking into the living room. She took a seat in the large, overstuffed armchair and stretched her leg out on the ottoman. Amelia could see her try to hide a satisfied smile, but she couldn't. Amelia hated to tell her grandmother that although Brian had told her about his old life, he was most definitely not interested in starting a new life. Not with Amelia, not with anyone. That no matter what Granny had seen out there on the porch, it meant nothing. Not to Brian. Not to Amelia, either. A few kisses, a few confidences. That's all.

After Amelia left, she'd be no more than a very small memory to him. And to her? She'd forget about him the minute she got onto the highway, which she hoped would be very soon.

"Considering what the doctor said, and how well you're doing, what would you think if I left tomorrow?" Amelia said lightly. *Don't make too much of it.* "There are problems at my office. But I won't leave if you think you can't manage on your own and with the home-help workers."

Granny's face paled. "Of course I can manage," she said. "That's no problem. Does this have anything to do with…?"

"It has to do with you and how much progress you've made. If I thought for one moment that you couldn't manage on your own…"

"But I can," Granny insisted, sitting up straight. "I just thought…"

"Things are not always what they seem," Amelia said, fearing Granny was going to go into the Brian situation, and wanting to head her off. "Now, what shall we have for dinner? How about a Caesar salad? I see you've washed the lettuce. I'll make the dressing and some croutons. I made it for Jeff one night. He loved it."

"Jeff is your…"

"My boyfriend," Amelia said firmly before correcting herself. "I mean, my almost fiancé." But the vision of Jeff in his three-piece suits and his button-down shirts left her feeling numb. She'd learned a lot in these few days, and the most important thing was that there was no future for her and Jeff. When she got back, she'd have to make that clear to him. She knew that now. It was one thing she had to thank

Brian for. He'd cleared up a few things in her mind. If she could get that excited by his kiss, she had no business thinking of marrying someone else. *Anyone* else. Which meant she would not be getting married anytime soon. Just as well.

She had work to do. She had no time for dating or riding roller coasters at county fairs or jumping up and down on pogo sticks. Her work was so challenging, and so much had gone wrong while she'd been away that she didn't see how she'd ever be able to take a vacation again.

"You'll be back, won't you?" Granny asked anxiously, as Amelia strode purposefully into the kitchen.

"Of course," Amelia said over her shoulder. "Call me if you need me."

"Does Brian know you're leaving?" Granny asked anxiously from the living room.

Amelia stuck her head around the corner. "I don't think he'll be surprised."

"But you'll say goodbye to him, won't you?"

"Of course." Not. Why bother? Why put them both through an embarrassingly awkward situation for no reason? What did Granny think would happen? He'd fall apart at the thought of her leaving? He'd beg her to stay? That he couldn't cope on his own? It was laughable, really.

Brian would only try to hide his relief at her departure while she tried to conceal the very real pain of knowing that he didn't care. Instead, she'd slip away in the morning after making sure Granny was all right. She'd phone the home-help people and make sure everything was on schedule, make sure Granny had everything she needed. She was sure Brian would continue to check in on his neighbor, just as he'd done before Amelia had come. He'd probably come even more often, knowing there was no chance he'd run into her.

Amelia managed to get through the dinner, though she had no idea how the salad and the fettuccine she'd cooked tasted. She and Granny made polite conversation. Granny made an effort to control her disappointment at the outcome of her matchmaking attempt, and Amelia pretended she'd never noticed. Amelia's mind was on her departure, on how to make it as painless as possible for her and Granny. If she left early enough, she could go straight to her office and start sorting out the mess. She told herself to focus on that and nothing else.

The next morning, she had time to call the home-help people and tell them she was leaving. They assured her they'd continue on their three-times-a-week schedule, and told her that Granny was making excellent progress.

But Amelia didn't like the way Granny looked that morning. Her grandmother's smile was forced, and her eyes filled with tears when Amelia kissed her goodbye.

"I'll be back," Amelia promised. "If you need me, just give me a call."

Granny nodded. "I'm fine. Don't worry about me. Thank you, dear. It was so lovely to see you." Then she choked up and couldn't say anything else.

Amelia blinked back the tears. If she didn't leave now, she'd never leave. Filled with guilt and riddled with second thoughts, she drove slowly down the road toward the highway. At the intersection of the two country roads, she saw a man dressed in baggy shorts and an old, ripped T-shirt. Brian! Her heart pounded. She'd hoped to get out of the area without another meeting. Damn, damn, damn. What was he doing out here?

She stopped the car. After all, she couldn't just drive past and leave him in a cloud of dust, no matter how much she wanted to. But she kept the motor running.

"You're out early," he said. He glanced in the back seat, where Amelia's laptop computer was piled on top of a stack of file folders. He frowned.

"I…I'm leaving."

"Back to the city," he said, his mouth in a tight line. "I'm not surprised."

"Granny's much better. You heard what the doctor said. She doesn't need me. My office, on the other hand, does need me."

"So that's what it's all about?" he asked, his eyes hard and steely. "Work comes first. Family last."

"Look," she said over the purr of the engine, "I came to take care of my grandmother. I put her first. Does she want me to stay longer? Yes. Would I like to stay on? Of course. But I have a job. I have responsibilities. So I have to ask myself, does my grandmother really need my help? No. You know as well as I do that I don't belong here. I don't live here. If you think I'm leaving because I need to be needed, maybe you're right. But don't go reading too much into the obvious."

"What's obvious is that, lately, you've seemed like a different person than the woman who barged in on me that first day."

"Barge? I did not barge."

He raised his arms. "Whatever. What I'm trying to say is that the country seemed to agree with you. You seemed relaxed, more carefree, mellow."

She stared at him in disbelief. Had he really given her a compliment? "Well, thank you, I think," she said at last.

"That's not all. As you've noticed, I have started working again, and I have you to thank for it." He paused and braced his arms against the car and leaned down. His face was only inches from hers. "I can't believe you were going to leave without saying goodbye."

She bit her lip. How could she deny it? How could she deny that her heart was beating frantically, that her hands were shaking so badly, she'd wrapped her fingers tightly around the steering wheel so he wouldn't notice. Even now, knowing that he wasn't interested in her, she wanted to look deep into his eyes to see if there was something there, something that could make her change her mind about him. Most of all, she wanted to know if he really cared that she was leaving. Before she could ask, he straightened.

"I thought we were friends," he added. "I'll miss you. But I'll get over it. I always do."

She blinked. His bitterness shouldn't surprise her. She was leaving just like his wife had. Only she was *not* his wife. Not his anything. She didn't know what to say. She didn't plan on missing him. Not at all. But then, he was alone in the country while she'd be back in the midst of things. There was no way she was going to miss him, and she didn't intend to lie about it just to be polite.

"Good luck," she said. That was safe.

"Thanks." He stepped back and she pulled away. In the rearview mirror she could see him standing there in the road, watching her drive away. Why she should have a hollow feeling in the middle of her chest, she didn't know. Turning onto the highway, she felt a huge surge of relief. She wouldn't have to see him again. She wouldn't have to be afraid of running into him at Granny's or in town. She'd be able to stand in front of her open window at dawn in San

Francisco without the possibility of looking down to see him and his truck parked below.

When she got back, instead of going straight to the office, she went home. The apartment, with its view of the bridge and the bay, seemed cold and empty, despite the fact that the cleaning lady had been there and turned on the heat for her. She called Granny, and when she heard her grandmother's voice, her eyes filled with tears. What on earth was wrong with her? Granny sounded positively cheerful. No words of blame or regret.

"Are you sure you're okay?" Amelia asked.

"Of course. I'm just fine. Brian is here. We're having a cup of tea together."

"How nice," Amelia said, her pulse accelerating for no reason at all—other than she could picture Brian sitting at Granny's table, with his broad shoulders and long legs seeming to take up the whole room. She wondered what his expression had been on hearing she'd called. Had he frowned? Had he gotten up and left the room? Had he let one of those half smiles tilt the corner of his mouth? Was he going to ask to talk to her? If so, what should she say?

There was a long silence. Amelia didn't know what else to say, and apparently Granny didn't, either. Amelia wondered if they'd talked about her.

Brian wouldn't dare say anything negative about her, or Granny would leap to her defense, wouldn't she?

"How are things at work?" Granny asked finally.

"Oh, I haven't checked yet. I'm sure everything will work out. I was tired, so I came straight home." But *tired* wasn't exactly the word for what Amelia was feeling. She was let down, restless and out of sorts. She thought she'd be glad to be home, but when she opened the window and breathed in the brisk San Francisco air, the noise of the traffic was jarring, and she closed the window with a sharp bang.

"Brian says to say hello," Granny said.

Amelia swallowed hard. What was she supposed to say to that? "Okay, well, I'll let you go," Amelia said.

"Goodbye, dear, and thank you so much for coming up to take care of me. I hope you'll come back sometime when I'm more fun."

"Granny, you're always fun. I had a great time. I will come back." But would she? Not if Brian Wolf was still in the neighborhood.

Brian left Helen's house and took a long walk in the woods with his dog.

"So she's gone," he said. "She's back where she belongs. Didn't I tell you she wouldn't last?"

Dante barked his assent as they scrambled down a steep trail. Brian had to admit that Amelia's visit had changed him. He'd actually started working again. How had she done it? Unlike others, she'd never told him to start work. She didn't bribe or threaten him. She'd just shown interest. He'd thought she was sincere.

Hell, he'd thought she was a lot more than sincere. He'd thought she was beautiful, sexy, edgy, warm, exciting. And, damn it, he missed her. How could that be? He barely knew her. She'd only been here for a matter of days, and she'd only been gone a few hours. He'd been fine before she came, he'd be fine now that she'd left. But he wasn't fine now. He wasn't able to do anything—not work, not split wood, not read or surf the Internet. His mind was in turmoil. Was it just because she'd left?

Why *had* she left so suddenly? Because he'd been honest with her? Because he'd told her he would never love again? Why would she care? She'd seemed interested in him, yes, but that was only because she didn't know him.

When she'd called her grandmother, it was all he could do to keep from grabbing the phone and telling her…what? What could he have said that would make any sense? I miss you? I wish you hadn't left? There's an ache in my gut that I can't get rid of, and it's all your fault? You had to come up here and show me that all women aren't the same? But she was the same. She couldn't wait to get back to her real life. But was that because of what he'd told her? He knew that he wasn't capable of loving a woman the way she should be loved. No, his work had always come first.

But not now. Now his work held as little interest as it had before she'd arrived.

"What's wrong with me?" he asked Dante. "I spoil everything with Amelia by telling her the truth about how much my work means to me, and yet, I can't force myself to get back to my computer or to my shop."

Dante stopped and looked at him, his head tilted to one side as if he were just as perplexed as Brian was. His eyes were warm and sympathetic. Brian rubbed his head. "Thanks, buddy," he said drily. "I appreciate your empathy. But what I need is advice. What should I do? Never mind, I know the answer. Pretend she never came. Roll back the clock to that day she stumbled on our place. Amelia with her hair like polished brass and her high heels and her attitude. Why didn't you scare her off then? No, you had to fall for her. If you hadn't, we wouldn't be in the place we are now. If you'd barked, snarled, jumped on her, she would have run away. But there was something about her, wasn't there? Something that lingers and gets to you. The smell of her hair in the sunshine, the sound of her voice, the dark bedroom window over there. Why does everything remind me of her? Never mind. You don't know the answers any more than I do. We'll give it a day or two. Then we'll see. You can be sure of one thing—she's not thinking about us. You heard that phone conversation with Helen? She never asked about us. Why? Because she doesn't care. She's already forgotten us. Just like we're going to forget her."

Chapter Nine

Amelia had thought it would be painful to tell Jeff she wasn't going to marry him. He looked shocked, but not hurt.

"I don't get it," he said over coffee after work a few days after she'd returned from the country. "What happened up there in the country?"

"Nothing, why?" Amelia crossed her fingers in her lap to keep from being struck by lightning for lying. Something *had* happened up there in the country. She'd fallen for a man who had no intention of falling for anyone ever again. Especially not her. The good thing was that no one knew. No one suspected that she'd fallen in love all by herself. Love? Could a person fall in love in a few days? Okay, maybe it wasn't love. But if it wasn't, it would have to do until the real thing came along.

Love or lust, whatever it was, was sad when it was one-sided. So sad, she felt like lying down and having a good cry. It was actually worse than sad. It was pathetic, and it was downright stupid. But there it was.

"When you left here I thought we had an understanding," Jeff said with a look of total confusion.

Amelia took a deep breath. "I was going to think it over. I did, and I decided it wasn't going to work."

"But why? We have so much in common." He reached for her hand across the table and squeezed it lightly.

Amelia felt nothing but annoyed. She pulled her hand back. She wished he could just accept the fact that she wasn't that interested in him. She had really misled him, and for that, she was truly sorry, because she knew how that felt.

"That's not enough," she said. She knew that now. Just one kiss from someone else had told her she wanted more than compatibility.

"Not enough?" Jeff said incredulously. "What more do you want?"

What she wanted was thrills. She wanted excitement. She wanted to be surprised. She wanted to go back on the roller coaster, to bury her face against Brian's shoulder, to feel his arm around her. She wanted to fly through the air, her heart in her throat.

She wanted to hear the screams of joy. She wanted to get on the roller coaster of life, go through its ups and downs with someone at her side who understood her. She wanted to jump up and down on a pogo stick, to feel young again, or rather, young for the first time in her life.

What she didn't want was to marry a predictable man. It was more than that. She didn't want a predictable job, either. She'd straightened out everything at her office and settled the dispute with F and F, but just a few days later, she found the work to be boring. What on earth was wrong with her? She suddenly realized Jeff was looking at her intently, waiting for her answer.

"What do I want? I don't know. I wish I did. Maybe I need a different job or a change of scenery."

"You just had a change of scenery. You went up to the country. You haven't been the same since."

"Maybe that's a good thing," she mused, half to herself. Brian's words echoed in her brain. *More mellow, relaxed, carefree.* These days, she felt anything but. She felt anxious, stressed and nervous. Now that she'd told Jeff, she thought she'd at least feel relieved.

"A good thing? How can you say that? When you left, you enjoyed your work and you and I got along perfectly. Now, by your own admission, you're not happy with anything."

"Not here, no," she murmured. She looked out

the window of the coffee shop at the cars whizzing by, and instead she saw a bucolic scene—Granny's roses and clear skies and the breeze whispering through the pine trees. And the face of her neighbor, the set of his shoulders, the wry half smile on his face, his lips on hers, their kisses. She gave a little involuntary shiver.

"I know," he said, beaming proudly. "We'll take a vacation together. We'll go on a cruise to Mexico. We'll dance till dawn, we'll dine at the captain's table, we'll play blackjack and we'll sign up for the glass-bottom boat off Baja."

Amelia stared at him in disbelief, as if he'd suggested crossing the country in a covered wagon. How little he knew her. Or more accurately, how little he knew the person she'd become. How could he know the new her? She didn't know herself very well, either, anymore. "I don't think so, Jeff," she said gently. "I'm sorry, but I'm not very good company these days. You go. Take someone else."

"I don't get it," he said, shaking his head. "You're a different person than you used to be. You've changed and I haven't. It's over for us isn't it?"

He was more perceptive than she'd realized, because she *had* changed and it *was* over. She put some money on the table and stood up.

"Yes, it is, Jeff. I'm sorry," she said.

When Amelia got home, turned on her computer

and tried to work, she stared at the screen as if the words were in a foreign language. She pressed her fingers against her temples, as if she could stimulate her brain that way, but it didn't work. Next, she picked up the newspaper, sank down in an easy chair and thumbed through the pages without knowing what she was reading. Finally, her eyes lit on an article about the exhibition at the San Francisco Children's Toy Museum.

She remembered that unopened letter from the museum she'd seen at Brian's house. Had he ever opened it? Would he have considered going to the exhibit? She knew the answers to those questions. They were no and no. It was too bad. It would be so good for him to get out of his rut, see some new toys, maybe even display his toys. It would be a psychological boost, and it would get his name out and remind people that he was still alive, and still creating new products. But he wouldn't leave Pine Mountain; she was sure of that. And whatever he did or didn't do had nothing to do with her.

It was time to stop thinking about him and get on with her life. One thing she'd never done before was visit a children's museum. She had no kids, and saw none in her future. Especially after she'd just turned down the one man she thought she might marry.

But she cut out the article and pinned it to her bulletin board. She wondered what kind of toys were popular these days, besides the ones Brian had invented and the obvious electronic ones. She wondered if there would be anything there to compare with his miniature roller coaster or his pogo stick. And if there was, what would kids think?

Brian shoved his pile of unanswered mail into a bag to throw in the garbage. If anyone had anything important to say to him, they could e-mail him or call him on the phone. Not that he ever answered his phone, but his machine would pick up and he could answer or not. Mostly not. One envelope fell to the side. Just out of curiosity, he opened it. He went out on his deck and stared off into the distant valley for a long time. Then he stuffed it into his pocket, whistled for his dog and walked over to Helen's house.

"What would you think of taking care of Dante for me for a few days?" he asked Helen.

Helen reached down to pet the dog at her feet. "You know I'd love it," she said. "Don't tell her I said so, but I've been lonely ever since Amelia left. I'd welcome the company. Have you, um, talked to her?"

"Amelia? No," he said shortly. What would he tell Amelia? That he, too, had been lonely since she'd left? That he missed her? That he couldn't work, sleep or do much of anything, and that it was her fault?

"Where are you going?" Helen asked.

"To San Francisco. I've been invited to speak at a symposium of toy makers at a museum."

"But, Brian…"

"I know what you're going to say," he said. "I never go to those things. But maybe it's time I did."

"Yes, definitely," she said, her eyes wide, a big smile on her face. He knew what she was thinking, and he wished she wouldn't. He didn't want her to get her hopes up. He had no idea what Amelia had told her grandmother. He could only imagine it went something like this: "I have to get away. The country is too boring. Your neighbor is the most boring man I've ever met."

"I'd rather Amelia didn't know I was going to the city," he said.

"My lips are sealed," she said, drawing an imaginary line across her mouth. "You can count on me. It's just, well…never mind."

"What is it?"

"I wanted to send her my grandmother's Wedgwood pitcher for her birthday."

"Is it her birthday?"

"Oh, yes, didn't she tell you? I should have given it to her when she was here, but I forgot. Now I'm afraid to mail it. It's very valuable, and very fragile."

"Maybe I could leave it at her office," he suggested. Leave it with a receptionist and flee the premises before she saw him. She'd think he'd come to see her, and he didn't want to mislead her again. That's where he'd gotten in trouble the last time.

"That's a wonderful idea," Helen said brightly. "I'll wrap it up right now. When are you going?"

Brian checked into a hotel in the downtown area of the big city that represented everything he didn't like. He stood at the window of his room on the nineteenth floor to survey the scene. He was high enough so the traffic noise was muted, and he had to admit the view of the sun setting over the Golden Gate Bridge was spectacular. The panel discussion was tomorrow, and he had nothing official to do tonight.

He knew what he wanted to do. He wanted to see Amelia. He wanted to see her in her setting. At her work, with her fiancé or at a trendy bar with co-workers. He wanted to see her as he'd seen her that first day, in a suit and high heels, her red hair fashionably styled. This way, he would know for sure she didn't belong in the country. He'd know there was no chance she could be happy there. No possibility he could convince her to come back.

Because unless he saw her like that, he'd have the memories stuck in his brain of Amelia riding a roller coaster, Amelia rolling around in the leaves under the apple tree, Amelia with a smudge of flour on her nose. And he'd wonder, he'd always wonder, what would have happened if he'd asked her to stay. If he'd told her how he felt about her. If he'd said that he knew she was nothing like his ex-wife. If he'd begged her to give him a chance. If he'd said that he was ready—or he could be ready, with her help—for a new life.

He'd thought that as soon as she'd left, the images would fade. But no, they were more vivid than ever. They encouraged him to believe in something that was unbelievable. That Amelia felt something for him. Something that he'd seen in her eyes, heard in her voice. He didn't know what to call it—it couldn't be love. He also wanted to believe that these feelings he couldn't shake—the sleepless nights, the inability to concentrate on anything—meant that he'd turned the corner and was ready to live again and, best of all, to love again.

So he went out on the town. He strolled up and down Union Street, all over Cow Hollow, standing in the doorways of restaurants and bars, watching and listening to music, to yuppies laughing, drinking and talking. But she wasn't there. He was half relieved, half disappointed. He had her home address as well as her office address in his pocket—Helen had seen to that. "So you can deliver the pitcher, but only if you have the time," she'd said when he'd dropped off Dante that morning.

So why didn't he? Why didn't he call her like a normal person, tell her he had something for her and drop it off? She'd recognize it right away for the setup it was, and they'd have a good chuckle over Helen's refusal to give up on them. He didn't know why he didn't call her and go see her. Maybe he wasn't ready for a face-to-face meeting.

He continued walking until he came to her building, a charming duplex painted gray and white. He looked up at her window. There was a light on, but he saw no one. He stood there for many minutes, picturing her in her kitchen. Did she bake pies in the city? Probably not. He imagined her in her bedroom, wearing that nightgown he'd seen her in at her grandmother's that morning, and he clenched his fist around the paper her address was written on. His pulse leapt, the way it had that morning. Maybe she was there with her almost fiancé. The idea made him feel sick.

He walked up the front steps and looked at the mailbox and the buzzer with *Tucker* written next to it. He took a deep breath and pressed the buzzer. He had an insane desire to run before she could let him in. But he had an even stronger desire to stay, and an overwhelming need to see her, to talk to her. He waited an eternity but no one answered. Of course not. Why would she be in on a Saturday night? If she wasn't at a restaurant or a bar, maybe she was at a movie or at the symphony with her fiancé. Or out celebrating her birthday. Of course, that was it. She'd be surrounded by throngs of friends. How could he compete with that?

He ground his teeth in frustration. He hadn't come to the city to see her, and yet now that he was here, he wondered what was the point of this trip if he didn't? Sure, he would connect with the world of toys again, but was that enough?

It had to be. He'd tell Helen he'd tried but hadn't been able to get in touch with her.

Amelia yanked on the cord of the vacuum cleaner, and the roar in her ears died down. She'd finally stopped her Saturday-night cleaning binge. She didn't know what was wrong with her. She had a cleaning lady who came once a week, but for some reason, she was attacking her apartment like a woman possessed. She'd turned down three invitations that evening—she just couldn't face another singles' scene. Not that she wanted to face a married scene, either, especially not with Jeff. Tonight, she only wanted to stay home with her dust rag and her thoughts. She'd go to the museum tomorrow and look at toys, and after that, she would wash her hands of anything and everything connected with Brian Wolf.

The Children's Toy Museum of San Francisco was located in a spacious, old Victorian house in Pacific Heights that had been donated by a wealthy family. Walls had been ripped out to make three floors of space for exhibits. There had been no attempt to fill it with e-toys. The house was old-fashioned, as were most of the toys. There were no video games. But everywhere there were signs that said Please Touch.

Not that the toys didn't make use of the latest technology—like a robot that looked like a dog. Amelia lingered, watching children lead the robot around. Then there was the pièce de résistance—at least, for her—the toy kitchen stove where the food turned color when it was done. Amelia remembered that Brian had invented it. Fascinated, she watched while a docent helped a little girl make a tiny cake, patting it with her little pudgy fingers and putting it in the oven. Amelia felt a surge of pride, almost as if *she'd* invented the stove. Brian should be here. He should see this. But he was far away, hidden behind a tall fence, reveling in his solitude. Watching these kids play, she felt a pang of loss for her own childhood. Could she make it up by raising her own children in a different way? She certainly understood Brian's disappointment at not having his own kids and watching them enjoy the toys.

"You could even bake an apple pie in it."

Amelia wheeled around and her knees buckled. It was him. She wasn't prepared to see him, or for the chills that ran up her spine or the way her face flamed.

"I came to see the toys," she blurted, then wished she had bitten her tongue. She hadn't prepared herself for this meeting because she thought it would never happen. So she'd blurted a blatant lie, and he must have known it. The truth was, she'd come to see him, hoped to see him, hoped that he'd made the effort to come to the city, because if he hadn't...

But he had made the effort. He'd come to town, yes, but he hadn't bothered to look her up. That almost made it worse. That hurt.

"What do you think?" he asked, crossing his arms over his chest.

"I think you could have called me. Oh, you mean the toys. They're amazing," she said, tearing her eyes from his face to look around at the toys. "The best part is watching the kids. You should be very proud."

"I am," he said. Then he looked at his watch. "I'm supposed to be on a panel discussing—guess what?—toys. I don't suppose you'd want to... No, you'd be bored."

"I'd like to come," she said. No matter that he hadn't made an attempt to see her, he was not going to get rid of her that fast. She was not going to simply fade away. At least he'd come to the city. That was a big step. She needed to find out just how big, and how many more steps he'd be willing to take.

She sat in the back of the lecture room on the third floor, along with a mixture of parents, squirming kids and toy-industry types, and heard Brian being introduced. Some of the words they used that stuck in her brain were *brilliant, innovative, amazing.* Brian looked embarrassed at all this praise. Then he stood and talked about the future of toys. He spoke with passion and humor and intelligence. She was mesmerized. This was the man who'd been hiding behind a tall fence. This was a man who seemed more and more at ease as the session went on. This was the man she'd fallen in love with. She stared at him, shocked at the conclusion she'd just come to.

She sat on the edge of her seat, excited and encouraged that he was focusing on the future and not the past. After the discussion, many people went up to ask questions. He caught her eye and mouthed, "Wait" to her. As if she'd leave now. Even if he just wanted to say goodbye, she had no intention of walking out of that room without talking to him. For all she knew, his plan was to jump in his car and head back to Pine Mountain immediately so he wouldn't have to spend another minute in the admittedly noisy, hectic city.

When the room finally emptied of all but a few people, Brian excused himself and strode across the room to where Amelia was waiting. He'd never lost sight of her, never stopped thinking about her, even during the discussion. He wondered if, and how, he'd managed to sound coherent and knowledgeable about anything with her in the back row. He couldn't believe she'd stayed through the whole thing. If she hadn't, if she'd gotten up and walked out—and he wouldn't have blamed her if she had—he would have had to go after her. Because he had to talk to her.

Seeing her there at the museum this morning had sent his heart pounding. He could no longer fool himself into thinking he'd come to the city for the toys or for the museum. He'd come for her.

"Amelia, we need to talk. Where can we go?"

"How about the Top of the Mark Hopkins Hotel? There's a wonderful view from up there. On a clear day, you can see forever."

"I don't need to see forever. All I want to see is you."

She nodded. He wasn't sure if she believed him. He had to convince her. He wasn't going home until she'd at least given him a chance.

She drove through the streets with great skill, weaving through the traffic until she pulled up in the hotel parking lot. It was crystal clear to him that she was at home here. What chance did he have of persuading her to move to the country?

They rode up in the glassed-in outdoor elevator. They were the only passengers. Instead of admiring the stunning view of dusk settling on the shimmering waters of the bay, and of the bridge with its lights on, she didn't even appear to notice it. Instead, she turned to look at him.

"Why didn't you tell me you were coming to town?" she asked.

"Last-minute decision. By the way, your grand-mother sent you a birthday present."

She laughed. "My birthday is in January. So she hasn't quit hoping."

"Neither have I," he said solemnly.

She didn't say anything, but her brown eyes dark-ened. She leaned back against the wall, her lips pressed together as if she was afraid of saying something.

"You know, I don't have much of a track record in relationships," he said.

"You're not the only one," she murmured.

"You mean you and Jeff…?"

She shook her head. "I broke up with him."

He felt a huge wave of relief. He hadn't known. He'd been afraid to ask.

The elevator came to a halt on the top floor. The doors opened. No one got in. He didn't want to change venues—if they did, he might lose his nerve. So he put his finger on the button for the lobby, and they started back down. She didn't seem to notice.

"I didn't come to the city because I was invited to the museum today."

Her eyes widened. Either she was surprised or she didn't believe him, or both.

"I came to see you."

"But you said—"

"I know what I said. That my work came first. But after you left, I couldn't work. I need you."

"Me?" She looked stunned. Her face paled, and she gripped the rail along the side of the elevator. He had a momentary feeling of panic. What if she didn't want to hear this? What if she wanted nothing more than to escape from these glass walls? He couldn't tell. But he had to go on until he'd said everything. He had to give it his all before he gave up and went home empty-handed.

"You. I used to live for my work. Inventing was my first love. I believed that, even when I couldn't make myself continue. Then you came along…."

"And barged onto your property," she said with a smile tilting one corner of her mouth.

"Yes. No. Whatever you did, you shook up my world. You made me start thinking about something, someone, besides myself."

"And that's why you're here today?"

"Yes."

"You said you hadn't changed."

"I was wrong. I have changed. Maybe not enough, but…"

"Enough for what?" she asked. They reached the lobby. The doors opened and a crowd of people got in the elevator. He and Amelia stepped back, and were squeezed together against the far wall. He put his arms around her waist. He inhaled the sweet scent of her hair. She sighed softly and his hopes rose. She hadn't pushed him away. Maybe she couldn't, given the circumstances. Maybe she would have if there'd been more room.

They rode back up again, this time without speaking, just listening to the inane conversation going on around them.

"Wow, what a view!"

"Don't stand too close to the window."

"Look, there's the Golden Gate Bridge."

This time, they got out on the top floor and went into the restaurant. After they'd ordered a bottle of white wine, he said, "Where were we?"

"You said you'd changed," she reminded him.

"I have. And so have you." He reached across the table and took her soft hands in his. "What do you think, is there any hope for you and me?"

"For you and me," she repeated. "As in…"

"As in, you and me together…forever."

"Brian…"

"Don't say no. Think it over. If you don't want to live in the country, we'll live here." He waved one hand toward the view out the window. "It's a beautiful city."

She stared at him as if he'd suggested living on Mars. He grinned at her. "What's wrong? You think I'm some kind of country yokel who couldn't fit in here?"

"No, no, of course not, I just… Give me a few minutes to digest this." She took a sip of her wine, then set the glass down unsteadily, as he watched anxiously. He could almost see the wheels turning in her head. If she wouldn't live with him in the country *or* the city, what hope was there for them? None. Then it wasn't about geography, it was about something else. It must be because she didn't love him. He let her hands go and stretched his legs out in front of him.

"I didn't realize this would come as such a shock to you," he said ruefully.

"A shock? Why wouldn't I be shocked after you told me you were a lousy husband and a lousy lover, and now you're saying you want to try all over again, here in the city?"

"Well, of course, I was hoping you'd say you'd rather live in the country at my house."

"You were?"

With every word she said, his spirits sank deeper. What had made him think she felt the same way he did? Still, he refused to give up. He had another card to play—the grandmother card.

"You'd be near your grandmother. And you and I would go for long walks in the woods, pick berries, make love under the trees. You'd bake apple pies...."

"Who do you think I am, Betty Crocker?"

"No, no. You don't have to bake. You don't have to do anything. But if you want to do something, you can work with me or..."

Now her cheeks were flushed and her eyes were full of unshed tears.

"Amelia, for God's sake, don't cry. I'll shut up. I won't say another word. I've said way too much already. And all you've done is remind me of what an idiot I've been, what ridiculous things I've said to you."

Suddenly, her tears turned to laughter. She laughed softly at first, then louder. Finally, she had to press her hand against her mouth to force herself to stop.

"I…I'm sorry," Amelia said, glancing around the room to see if anyone had noticed her outburst. "What do you want me to say, Brian?" She honestly didn't know if he was proposing they move in together, that she quit her job to bake pies for him and that he'd changed enough…for what?

"Say whatever you want," he said. "Just tell me the truth. Frankly, I didn't expect you to cry or laugh, but whatever. At least I haven't bored you. What I was hoping you'd say was that you'd fallen in love with me the way I've fallen in love with you. I know—it's too soon. That's why I hope you won't say no, just say you'll give it some time."

"How much time?"

"Would five minutes be enough?" he said, looking at his watch. "Because I'm desperate. I love you, Amelia."

"All right," she said. Her head was spinning. She wanted to believe him, but she needed more time.

More than five minutes. "I'll quit my job. Don't make too much of it. I realized when I got back that I hate it. So it's no big sacrifice. But I'll hang on to my apartment, because it's rent-controlled. That way, you won't feel any pressure if it doesn't work out."

"Hey," he said, "don't worry about me. I can handle pressure. Just tell me one thing, truthfully—do you think you could ever fall in love with me?" He leaned across the table and looked into her eyes. She couldn't speak over the lump in her throat. They sat at the table for a long moment. When he couldn't take it another minute, he tossed a pile of bills on the table and took her arm, and they headed for the exit.

In the elevator on the way down, they were once again squeezed together in the corner. This time, he kissed her between the 32nd and the 24th floors, and she kissed him back between the 24th and the lobby, only somewhat oblivious to the knowing looks and smirks from the other passengers.

She put her all into that kiss. It was a kiss that said what she couldn't say in words. That she loved him, she wanted him and she'd go anywhere with him. She thought he'd get the message, but apparently he still needed confirmation.

"Is that a yes?" he asked, slanting an intense look at her as they crossed the lobby, hand in hand.

"Yes, yes, yes," she said, stopping abruptly under the ornate chandelier in the middle of the high-ceilinged lobby. "I love you, Brian. I fell in love with you the day you took me on the roller coaster."

"Uh-oh. Life won't always be as exciting as a roller-coaster ride," he said.

"That's okay. The best part was having your arm around me, knowing you were there for me. That's what I've missed."

He hugged her to him, and they went out into the dark city streets to ride the cable car, stroll Fisherman's Wharf and have dinner at a little Italian restaurant she knew.

Drunk with love and lust and the promise of an incredible, happy future, Amelia said good-night to Brian at her door.

"I can't wait to see the expression on Granny's face," she said.

"If we get an early start, you can see her face about noon. Can you wait that long?"

She threw her arms around him and kissed him, a kiss full of promise. A kiss that said she could only wait so long—so long to tell Granny they were in love and getting married and living happily ever after, right next door.

It was almost noon the next day when they arrived at Granny's cottage in the woods. She was out in her garden, her legs propped up on a stool, her face tilted to the sun.

Brian coughed discreetly as they opened her front gate.

"You two," she exclaimed, her mouth falling open in surprise. "What are you doing here?"

"I brought her back, Helen. She told me she couldn't live without me, so I took pity on her and brought her with me. Of course, I'll have to make a few sacrifices—clear out a few closets, that kind of thing."

"Wait, wait," Granny said, waving her hand at them. "Are you saying…?"

"I'm saying, we're getting married and living happily ever after. Little Red Riding Hood and the Big Bad Wolf—right next door. How does that sound?" Amelia asked.

"It sounds like a fairy tale come true."

* * * * *

*Be sure not to miss the next
enchanting title in the
FAIRY-TALE BRIDES miniseries.
Can a beautiful chef convince a brooding,
sexy tycoon that there's more to happiness
than making money? See how a thoroughly
modern Cinderella does that, and wins her
prince's heart and lives happily ever after,
too…in
CINDERELLIE!
By Carol Grace
July 2005*

International bestselling author

Lilian Darcy

returns to

SILHOUETTE *Romance*®

with

The Millionaire's Cinderella Wife

On sale June 2005, SR #1772

Praise for Lilian Darcy from *Romantic Times*:

"Darcy's writing is flawless and her way with tiny details gives insight into these charming characters."
The Boss's Baby Surprise, SR #1729

"Darcy weaves a multilayered story with strong characters who make for a fabulous read!"
Saving Cinderella, SR #1555

And in July, don't miss Lilian's next book in

SPECIAL EDITION™

The Father Factor
On sale July 2005, SSE #1696

If you enjoyed what you just read,
then we've got an offer you can't resist!

Take 2 bestselling love stories FREE!

Plus get a FREE surprise gift!

Clip this page and mail it to Silhouette Reader Service™

IN U.S.A.	IN CANADA
3010 Walden Ave.	P.O. Box 609
P.O. Box 1867	Fort Erie, Ontario
Buffalo, N.Y. 14240-1867	L2A 5X3

YES! Please send me 2 free Silhouette Romance® novels and my free surprise gift. After receiving them, if I don't wish to receive anymore, I can return the shipping statement marked cancel. If I don't cancel, I will receive 4 brand-new novels every month, before they're available in stores! In the U.S.A., bill me at the bargain price of $3.57 plus 25¢ shipping and handling per book and applicable sales tax, if any*. In Canada, bill me at the bargain price of $4.05 plus 25¢ shipping and handling per book and applicable taxes**. That's the complete price and a savings of at least 10% off the cover prices—what a great deal! I understand that accepting the 2 free books and gift places me under no obligation ever to buy any books. I can always return a shipment and cancel at any time. Even if I never buy another book from Silhouette, the 2 free books and gift are mine to keep forever.

210 SDN DZ7L
310 SDN DZ7M

Name	(PLEASE PRINT)	
Address	Apt.#	
City	State/Prov.	Zip/Postal Code

Not valid to current Silhouette Romance® subscribers.

Want to try two free books from another series?
Call 1-800-873-8635 or visit www.morefreebooks.com.

* Terms and prices subject to change without notice. Sales tax applicable in N.Y.
** Canadian residents will be charged applicable provincial taxes and GST.
   All orders subject to approval. Offer limited to one per household.
   ® are registered trademarks owned and used by the trademark owner and or its licensee.

SROM04R   ©2004 Harlequin Enterprises Limited